Old Acquaintance

A MARY O'REILLY PARANORMAL MYSTERY

(Book Nineteen)

by

Terri Reid

OLD ACQUAINTANCE

A MARY O'REILLY PARANORMAL MYSTERY
(BOOK 19)

by

Terri Reid

The author would like to thank all those who have contributed to the creation of this book: Richard Reid, Sarah Powers and, the always amazing, Hillary Gadd. She would like to also thank Peggy Hannah, John and Vicki Daley and Mark Buus.

She would also like to thank all of the wonderful readers who walk with her through Mary and Bradley's adventures and encourage her along the way. I hope we continue on this wonderful journey for a long time.

Prologue

Tiny, white lights sparkled, tinsel glittered, and the electric fireplace glowed warmly, sending shadows of flames on the gifts laying underneath the Christmas tree. The brightly-colored lights from outside the house were covered in several inches of snow, causing the shrubs to glow softly in the early morning darkness.

The house was quiet as the ten-year-old boy padded down the carpeted stairs from his bedroom to the living room where his target awaited. He carefully placed his feet on the outer edges of the stairs, avoiding any sounds of creaking wood. The last thing he wanted to do was wake any member of his family on this early Christmas morning.

The family cat, seeing young Tony, fled from its warm perch on the back of the sofa to the safety of the cold kitchen. Tony didn't even notice the animal's departure, because he was so focused on the items next to the tree.

He paused next to the dollhouse for his sisters. He had been able to pick the lock on his father's workroom and had watched the progress of the house as his father had painstakingly created a miniature replica of their own house, complete with carpet scraps and wallpaper pieces. The project had taken his father weeks to complete. "What a total waste of energy," Tony said disdainfully, sneering at the toy.

He glanced around the rest of the tree. There, in another corner, was the G.I. Joe doll his little brother had wanted, although why a boy would want a doll was a mystery to Tony. He continued to search, looking behind the couch and chair, and even searching in the other rooms, but the present he had asked for was not there.

An ember of rage smoldered in the pit of his belly. *I never get what I want*, he decided. *Mom and Dad are always unfair. They always give the younger kids everything. I hate them. I hate them all.*

He walked through the first floor into the kitchen and then found the door to the basement. Switching on the light, he walked down the stairs and unlocked his father's workroom. A basket of rags lay on a pile in one corner. Tony took a can of lighter fluid down from the shelf and soaked the rags thoroughly. Then he took a box of matches from the same shelf and lit the pile, smiling as the flames slowly caught and the soaked rags ignited. He made his way around the fire, closed the workroom door and then carried the can of lighter fluid and the matches back upstairs.

He slipped on his boots and took his coat off the rack near the back door. Then he walked back into the living room and emptied the rest of the container of lighter fluid onto the gifts underneath the tree. With great satisfaction, he set a match to the top of the dollhouse and watched with glee as it was consumed by fire.

The lower branches of the tree lay near the dollhouse, and they started to turn red. Then, suddenly, with a loud whoosh, the entire tree was encompassed with flames that spread to the drapes and then onto the wall.

Tony put the empty container and box of matches on the table in the front hallway. Then he quietly opened the door and let himself out. He buttoned his coat and walked to the middle of the front lawn, watching the fire spread throughout the house with growing delight. *I told them I wanted a bike for Christmas,* he thought. *They should have bought me a bike.*

Later that morning, as the firemen and ambulance drivers removed the charred remains of the family from the house, one young fireman rolled a bright red, Schwinn bike out of the garage, which was the only part of the home that hadn't been destroyed.

"This had a ribbon and a tag on it," the young man said, his heart breaking for the lone survivor of the housefire. "Are you Tony?"

Tony nodded and smiled at the man. "Thank you," he said. "It was just what I wanted."

The fireman was surprised at the joy in the child's face, especially after just seeing the ambulances leave with his entire family.

"I guess your parents wanted you to have a Merry Christmas," he said.

Tony shrugged. "They should have left it under the tree."

Chapter One

Christmas music was softly playing through the computer, and Mary was sorting through boxes of Christmas decorations. "Oh, this is really lovely," she said, picking up an antique, blown-glass ornament that shone with iridescent colors.

Bradley glanced over from the desk and smiled. Mary was on the floor in the middle of the living room, surrounded by boxes and totes of Christmas things. She had tinsel on her shoulder and a bit of glitter on her nose where she must have itched herself. There were piles of ornaments all over the floor, but there didn't seem to be any organization going on there at all. "That was from my great-grandmother on my dad's side," he said. "She brought it with her from Sweden."

"Sweden," Mary said in awe, studying it as she lifted it up and twirled it by the attached ribbon. "How cool is that?"

"So, which of your piles are you going to put it in?" he asked, a teasing smile on his face.

She glanced over at him, her eyes narrowing at the slight mocking in his voice. "I have a system here," she said defensively, waving her arm over the six different piles on the floor.

She placed the glass ornament on the first pile. "This pile is the 'we definitely use, but have to be careful with' pile," she explained.

"We have to be careful with?" Bradley asked.

Nodding, Mary picked the glass ornament up again. "You know, put them someplace on the tree where they can't get accidentally knocked off."

"Does that happen to you often?" he asked. "Spontaneous Christmas ornament projectiles?"

Rolling her eyes, she huffed with frustration. "Did you forget that this will be the first Christmas with a kitten in the house?" she asked. "Lucky has knocked things off every surface she can get onto. I'm thinking the Christmas tree will be just one more notch in her kitty collar."

"Okay, good point," he said, and then he pointed to the next pile. "What's this one?"

Mary put the glass ornament down and picked up a sturdy, wooden nutcracker ornament. "This is the 'nothing can hurt us" pile," she explained. "These ornaments can go on the bottom tier of the tree because they're indestructible."

"Trees have tiers?" Bradley asked.

She studied him for a moment. "I have to say, I'm shocked at your lack of Christmas tree education," she said, shaking her head. "Wow, you're pretty much demoted to minion elf."

"And what does a minion elf get to do?" he asked.

She shrugged. "Well, you obviously don't get to decorate trees if you don't even know about tiers. And I've seen your efforts at present wrapping, so we won't even go there," she replied, biting back a smile. "Your Christmas cookie decorating wasn't bad, but you ate more than you decorated."

"Hey, they were good. I couldn't help myself," he said.

"Self-control," she said, shaking her head. "That's the first rule of being an elf."

He slipped out of his chair, carefully made his way through the festive piles on the floor, sat down next to her and began massaging her back. He leaned over and whispered into her ear. "So, what does a minion elf get to do?" he asked.

She closed her eyes and sighed happily. "Oh, that feels so great," she said.

He continued to massage her, and she leaned forward until her belly stopped her.

"So, what does a minion elf get to do?" he repeated, rubbing her lower back.

"Well," she exhaled softly, "I was going to say pick up reindeer poop. But, now…" she moaned as his hands slipped up her back and he massaged her shoulders.

"Now?" he asked, a grin spreading across his face.

"Now, you can do anything you want to do," she whispered.

He slid his arms from her shoulders and pulled her back into his arms. He looked down at her and smiled. "Anything?"

She looked up at him, her heart filled with love. "Well, not anything," she smiled back. "At least not down here. We don't want to crush the ornaments."

He chuckled softly, the vibrations sending chills through Mary's body. "Why don't we go upstairs for some minion elf training?" he suggested, one eyebrow raised.

"Well, I really should…" Mary began.

He leaned down and nibbled on the side of her neck.

"Oh," she breathed, feeling the warmth spreading throughout her body. "You do that really well."

He lifted his head. "Upstairs?" he asked.

She nodded. "Oh, yes, upstairs."

He stood and took both of her hands to help her up, then pulled her into his arms. "I love you, head elf," he said.

"I love you…" she began when the door burst open.

"We should just cancel Christmas!" Clarissa exclaimed, dumping her backpack on the ground. "It's just a big, fat lie anyway."

Chapter Two

"Minion training is postponed," Bradley whispered to Mary with regret, and she nodded in agreement.

Carefully stepping around the piles of ornaments, Bradley walked over to Clarissa. "So, what happened today?" he asked.

With tear-filled eyes, she looked up at him. "On the bus, some of the older boys were talking," she said, her voice filled with emotion. "And they said there is no such thing as Santa Claus."

"Who were those boys?" Bradley asked. "I'm going to call—"

"Are those the same boys who don't believe in ghosts?" Mary asked, interrupting Bradley.

Clarissa turned to Mary and nodded.

Mary grinned. "Well, that proves how smart they are," she said, following Bradley's trail through the ornaments and making her way to Clarissa. "Why don't we go into the kitchen, grab a snack and discuss this." She smiled at Clarissa. "Well, that is, if your father left us any cookies."

A giggle from Clarissa eased both of her parents' hearts.

A few minutes later, they were seated around the table with glasses of milk and a plate of cookies to share.

Mary studied her nine-year-old daughter for a moment, then asked her a question. "Clarissa, what do you think about what those boys said? About Santa not being real?"

Lowering her eyes, Clarissa was silent for a few moments. Then she looked up, first meeting Bradley's eyes and then Mary's. "I think they're right," she said softly. "I don't think there really is a Santa Claus."

Nodding slowly, Mary smiled at her daughter. "Now, that answer tells me that you're ready for some truth about Santa Claus," she said. "There are two different ways to believe in Santa. One way is to believe like a child, that Santa brings all kinds of toys and goodies. That he rides in a sleigh pulled by reindeer and lives at the North Pole with elves."

She studied Clarissa. "Does that sound like the Santa you used to believe in?" she asked.

Clarissa sighed and nodded.

"And it's wonderful that you did believe in that Santa," Bradley said. "Because it gave us a chance to get you things and surprise you. We get to play Santa and watch the joy on your face on Christmas morning."

"So, you're not going to be happy on Christmas morning anymore?" Clarissa asked.

Mary chuckled and shook her head. "Actually, that's where the other belief in Santa comes in," she said. "Saint Nickolas was a very good man who lived a long time ago. He was wealthy, and he enjoyed using his wealth to bless others. He loved the story about Jesus being born and the wise men bringing gifts. So, on Christmas night, he would travel around his community and leave gifts for children so they too could remember the love and beauty of that special night."

"You know," Bradley said after biting a head off a reindeer. "Your mom knows Santa Claus personally."

Wide-eyed, Clarissa turned to Mary. "You do? You honestly do?" she asked.

Mary smiled and nodded. "But this is one of those family secrets," she said, lowering her voice, "that we can't share with the general public."

Used to family secrets, Clarissa nodded. "But you do know him?" she questioned.

"Yes, I do," she said. "I met him when I first moved to Freeport. It was my first Christmas here, and because of a storm, I couldn't go back home to Grandma and Grandpa O'Reilly."

"So, you were all alone at Christmas?" the little girl asked.

Mary placed her hand on Clarissa's head and stroked her soft hair. "I thought I was going to be alone," she confessed. "And I was pretty sad. But then I met Stanley and Rosie, and they helped me."

"So, they met Santa too?" Clarissa asked.

"Well, he was in the same room as they were," Mary said with a smile. "And Rosie said she felt something, but they couldn't see him because he's a spirit."

"Santa's a ghost?" Clarissa asked, cocking her head to the side. "I never knew that. How does he get all those toys and the reindeer and the elves if he's a ghost?"

"So, when he was alive, he was Santa Claus?" she asked.

"Yes. Yes, he was," she agreed. "And because he was so good, and because he loved the birth of Jesus so much, when he died, God gave him a special job. During the Christmas season, he visits the earth and helps all of us to feel the wonder and joy of the season."

"The spirit of Christmas?" Clarissa asked.

"Exactly," Mary said. "He, Santa Claus, is the Spirit of Christmas. He influences us to have good will towards each other and to remember what this celebration is all about."

Clarissa sighed softly. "So, he doesn't bring gifts," she said sadly.

"No, but he influences others to give gifts and share their love," Bradley said. "So, in a way, he does bring gifts."

"And he doesn't have a naughty and nice list?" she asked.

"No, he doesn't," Bradley said. "And I'm really sorry that you learned that because now I can't bribe you to be good with Santa anymore."

Clarissa chuckled. "But if I feel the Spirit of Christmas, I'll want to be good anyway, right?"

"Right," Mary said. "And the more you allow yourself to feel that spirit of goodwill and peace, the greater the joy and peace that will come from it."

"What does he look like?" Clarissa asked.

Mary thought back to the red-robed spirit with the glow of joy emanating from him. "Exactly what you'd think Santa looked like," she said. "But he has the light of love all around him."

"I think I like this Santa better than the other one," Clarissa decided. She picked up a cookie and took a bite. "It's realer."

Mary grinned at Bradley and then smiled at Clarissa. "Exactly," she said. "It's much realer."

Chapter Three

Lifting Clarissa up, Bradley watched his daughter place the angel on the very top of the tree. "Good job," he said when she secured it on the vertical branch.

She smiled at him. "This is the best Christmas tree I've ever had."

"I agree," Bradley replied, putting her back on the ground.

"Grandpa Stanley," Clarissa asked, "what do you think?"

Stanley walked over, placed his hands on his hips and studied the tree carefully, his face displaying serious concentration. Then he lifted one hand and stroked his chin thoughtfully. "Well, I was thinking that maybe the tree from 1953 coulda been a might better," he said slowly, but then he shook his head. "But now that I remember it, it tweren't quite as sparkly or as tall as this one."

He smiled at her. "Yes siree, this tree takes the cake."

Clarissa grinned and threw her arms around Stanley. "And you're real old," she said excitedly. "So, you'd know stuff."

Chuckling, Stanley bent down and wrapped his arms around the little girl. "Yes, indeed, I'm almost as old as Santa Claus," he said. "And I do know stuff."

Clarissa leaned back and looked at Stanley's beloved, wrinkled face. "My mom said that you met Santa Claus," she said. "But you didn't get to see him."

"She's right," he replied. "He was helping us get six little orphans back home where they belong." He paused, remembering the burnt remains of the orphanage and the six tiny ghosts who had waited years for Santa to come. "He was right there in the room, and he spoke to your mother."

"Like he knew her name?" Clarissa asked, impressed.

Stanley nodded. "Now, I ain't saying he knew her personally-like," he explained. "But I reckon he'd heard of her. Your mom here, she's pretty famous in the place where spirits hang out."

Clarissa turned and looked over to Mary. "Are you famous?" she asked.

Mary laughed and shook her head. "I doubt it," she said. "Santa was just helping me with a case, that's all."

"You worked with Santa?" Clarissa asked, her eyes widening with new respect for her mother. "So, you're like an elf?"

Stanley laughed out loud. "Biggest elf I've ever seen."

"Stanley," Rosie immediately chided him. "That's not nice. Mary's not big, she's pregnant."

"I wasn't saying she was fat. I was saying she was tall," he said, defending himself. "She ain't fat t'all. As a matter o' fact, I was going to get after her for not eating more. She's too skinny by half."

Mary grinned at Stanley, picked up a cookie and took a bite. "Better?" she asked with a wink.

He chuckled. "Iffen you get yourself a glass of milk, I'll be happier than a pig in mud."

"That's gross," Clarissa said.

Mary laughed and nodded at Stanley. "I will go right in and pour myself a glass of milk," she said. "Just to make you happy."

Still chuckling, she left the living room and walked into the kitchen. As she moved to open the refrigerator, out of the corner of her eye she saw a shadow dart from the corner of the room. She quickly turned and walked past the refrigerator to the far end of the kitchen. She looked all around the room, but nothing was there.

"That's odd," she said softly.

"What's odd?" Mike asked, appearing next to her.

She smiled at the angel. "I thought I saw something, a shadow, dart across the room," she said. "But I looked and couldn't find anything."

Mike didn't smile, but slowly studied the room.

"Okay, Mike, you're spooking me," she said, trying to keep her voice light.

He looked back at her and shrugged. "I guess I'm still wary about whatever was in the asylum," he said. "I'm worried that it might have followed us home."

"Okay, now you're not just spooking me, you're scaring me," she said. "What are the odds?"

He shrugged. "I don't know," he said. "Because I couldn't figure out what we were dealing with." Then he sighed and smiled. "And maybe I'm just being paranoid."

She nodded. "Well, it wouldn't hurt to be extra vigilant," she said.

"And it wouldn't hurt to see what we can find out about those former residents of the asylum," he replied, gazing around the room once more.

"Yes," she said slowly. "And Mike?"

He looked back down at her. "What do you need, sweetheart?"

"Could you guard Clarissa even more closely until we figure this out?" she asked. "If it's the thing from the asylum, Bradley and I have already faced it down once, but Clarissa…"

He smiled at her. "Don't worry," he said. "I'll put myself on double-time guardian angel duty." He looked beyond her towards the living room. "Are you going to mention anything to Bradley?"

She shook her head. "Not yet," she said. "It could have been just a shadow from a car passing by, and he's so nervous about Mikey's arrival that I don't think he could handle any more stress."

Shaking his head, he stepped closer. "He can handle it," he whispered. "And, if you want my advice, you'll mention it to him."

"Wow, this is serious," she said, her stomach tightening.

He laid his hand on her cheek, and she could feel the cold from his touch. "Not serious," he said, "just cautious."

But Mary thought his eyes told another story.

Chapter Four

Later that night, after the house was dark except for the sparkling lights of the Christmas tree, Mary crept from her bedroom down the stairs to the kitchen. She stopped at the foot of the steps and smiled, her gaze drawn to the popcorn strung haphazardly on the tree. Stanley and Rosie had insisted the tree needed an old-fashioned look to it. Unfortunately, more popcorn was eaten than strung, so only one strand lay in the middle of the tree, like a narrow belt on an oversized waistline.

Clarissa had fallen asleep almost immediately, and Mary was sure there were visions of sugarplums dancing in her head. Stanley and Rosie had left for their home soon after, and she and Bradley...

Her smile grew wider, and she sighed softly. There was nothing like snuggling in the dark with only the glow of the Christmas tree lighting the room. She slowly descended the last step and walked towards the kitchen. The glass of milk she'd forgotten to pour earlier that night was tempting her, as were the sugar cookies packed away in the cookie jar. She pulled open the refrigerator door and smiled. "Snuggling burns calories," she laughed as she took the milk carton out and put it on the counter.

She froze and stared into the living room. She could swear that something moved in there. She walked around the counter, towards the living room, and heard a soft giggle. It sounded like a child's voice, but there was something about it that sent chills down her spine. "Who's there?" she asked, walking to the entrance of the room.

The giggle repeated, this time clearer.

"I don't find this funny at all," she replied firmly, trying not to show her fear. "Now, if you want my help, you will show yourself."

She looked around and saw the branches of the Christmas tree shake. She started to step forward, but a sudden grip of instinctual fear held her back.

"Where my bike?" the voice asked in a sing-song manner.

"Your bike?" Mary asked, her voice shaking slightly. "I don't have your bike, and you have to go."

The giggle repeated, and then the voice called out, "Mary. Mary. I've found you."

Mary gripped the edge of the couch, her knees weakening beneath her. It was the voice from the asylum, and it was in her home.

"Mike," she whispered, her voice dry and her heart pounding against her chest, praying the guardian angel could sense her need. It was hard to form words, hard to push them out her mouth. "Mike. I need you."

"No one is going to help you," the young voice mocked. "It's just you and me this time."

Suddenly Mike was standing in front of her, facing the tree, his body glowing with a powerful light. "You will leave this house," he said. His voice, although calm, seemed to reverberate around the room. "And you will leave it now."

"I want Mary," the voice replied in a sulky tone.

"You can't have her," Mike said.

"Oh, yes, I can," the voice countered. "And you can't stop me."

Mike slowly glided forward until he was in front of the tree. "I don't think you realize who I am," he said softly, but his words held strength. "I can stop you."

There was a moment of silence, and the tree shook. "You can't be everywhere," the childish voice replied, and Mary shivered at the malevolence in it. "I will get my way. I always get my way."

Suddenly, it seemed to Mary there was more light and air in the room. She pushed herself away from the couch and moved closer to Mike. "Is he gone?" she whispered, looking around the room.

He nodded. "For now," he said. "Are you okay?"

She nodded. "Thank you," she said. "I was so frightened." She shook her head. "I'm never frightened like that. I'm not afraid of ghosts."

"This was more than just a ghost," he said.

"More?" she shook her head, confused. "Like what?"

"Like nothing I've ever encountered before," he replied.

"What haven't you encountered before?" Bradley asked from the bottom of the staircase.

Mike glanced over to Bradley but stayed next to Mary. "We had a strange encounter of the asylum kind," he said.

"The asylum?" Bradley asked, rushing to Mary's side. "Are you okay?"

She nodded again. "Yeah. Yes. Mike came and…" she stopped and looked at him. "What did you do?"

Mike grinned at her. "I just flexed my angelic muscles," he teased, trying to remove the fear from her eyes.

"How long is he gone?" Bradley asked.

The smile dropped from Mike's face. "I don't know," he said. "He was easily intimidated. And, there's something else about him."

"Like what?" Bradley asked.

"Like, I'm not sure, but I'd really like to call Ian in on this one," he said.

"Yeah, good idea. I'll just get my phone," Bradley said, starting to turn.

"No," Mike said. "You go upstairs with Mary and watch over Clarissa. I'll go talk to him in person, then I'll come back."

Then he turned to Mary. "You need to tell Bradley what happened tonight and what happened earlier this evening," he said.

"Something happened earlier?" Bradley asked. "Why didn't you tell me?"

She blushed and met his eyes. "I got distracted," she said, and then Bradley reddened slightly, too.

Mike chuckled softly. "Okay, no more distractions," he teased. "Go upstairs, watch over Clarissa, and I'll be back as soon as I can."

Chapter Five

"No! No, Gillian! No!" Ian shouted as he thrashed around in his bed, his arms reaching out. "I'm coming. I'm coming."

Mike stood at the edge of the bed, watching his friend in the throes of an awful nightmare and wondering if he should wake him. Ian's face was filled with anguish, and there were tears flowing freely down his face.

"Gillian!" Ian suddenly screamed and immediately sat up in his bed, the blankets pooling around his waist.

He stared blindly into the room for a moment, and Mike realized he was still half-asleep.

"Are you okay?" Mike finally whispered.

Ian slowly turned his head towards Mike. "Can you save her?" he asked, confused.

"Dude, I can try," Mike said. "Where is she?"

Shaking his head, Ian dismissed the last dregs of his nightmare from his mind, and his eyes cleared. "I'm so sorry," he said hoarsely. "I've had a bit of trouble with my dreams lately."

"No," Mike said, gliding closer. "Don't apologize. Is everything okay? Is there anything I can do?"

Ian smiled bitterly. "Aye, well, I don't think this fits into your job description," he said. "But if for some reason I discover you can help, I promise I'll be calling."

Then his eyes narrowed, and Ian cocked his head. "Why are you here?"

"It's Mary," Mike began.

"The baby?" Ian asked immediately.

Mike shook his head. "No. No, the baby's fine," he said. "But I think whatever we encountered at the asylum followed her home. It visited her tonight."

Ian studied Mike. "And just what aren't you telling me?" he asked.

Mike sighed, shook his head and glided around the room slowly. "I can't get a read on it," he said. "It's not a demon. I can tell that much. But it's pretty powerful and…" He turned back to Ian. "Dangerous. Very dangerous."

Ian stood up and walked across the room to his closet, pulling jeans from a shelf and slipping them on.

"Wait, you don't have to leave now," Mike said. "I—"

"No, I'm fine," Ian said quickly. "I find my sleep has lately been interrupted by nightmares, and I'd just as soon not face them again."

He slipped on a shirt, then pulled a gym bag down and started putting extra clothing in it. Mike was torn. He knew that Ian had the skills to discover what this entity now haunting Mary was, but he couldn't get the image of Ian's grief-stricken face out of his mind.

"Is something wrong with Gillian?" Mike finally asked. "Do you need to stay? Do you need my help?"

Ian stopped packing for a moment and turned to Mike. "Aye, there's something wrong," he admitted sadly. "But there's naught I, nor anyone else, can do at the moment. It's all a waiting game for now."

"Are you sure?" Mike asked. "I don't want to take you away…"

Ian laughed, but the sound was bitter. "I'd rather be helping than sitting here feeling sorry for myself," he said. "Besides, I know you wouldna left their side unless it was urgent."

Mike nodded. "It's urgent, and I'm worried," he said. "But…"

Ian shook his head. "No," he said. "It's actually a boon for me. I'm a wee bit muddled, and this will give me the chance to clear my brain. So, it's thanks I should be giving to you."

Mike smiled at his friend. "I'll put in a good word upstairs for you," he said.

Ian smiled wanly. "Aye, I can use all the help and good will I can get," he said.

"Okay, I'm going to go back," Mike said. "I'll let them know you'll be there in a couple of hours."

Ian nodded. "Aye, the traffic should be light this time of night," he said. "I'll be there as soon as I can."

"Thank you," Mike said as he slowly faded away.

Ian stared at the spot Mike had just occupied and sighed slowly. "No. Thank you," he said softly. "Truly."

Chapter Six

Mary and Bradley sat on the window seat in Clarissa's room, Bradley's arm around Mary's shoulder, holding her close to his side. They stared in silence at their daughter sleeping peacefully underneath the quilt her mother, Jeannine, had started and the other women in her life had completed for her birthday. The adolescent kitten, Lucky, was curled up next to her, sharing the pillow.

"What do we do?" Bradley finally whispered.

"We fight it," Mary replied quietly, sitting up and facing him. "We fight it and we don't let it win."

Bradley shook his head. "No. What do we do once Mikey is born?" he asked. "How are you going to handle all of this and a baby?"

She leaned back against him and sighed. "I don't know," she said, placing her hands protectively on her belly. "I've sat up nights thinking about that very question. I just don't know."

He nodded and turned and placed a kiss on her head. "We're a team," he said. "Remember that. We're a team and I'll do whatever I can."

She glanced up at him. "It changes everything, doesn't it?" she asked. "Being a parent? It changes everything."

"Yes, it does," he replied, his eyes focused on the little girl in front of them. "Or, at least, it should."

"I've never felt so…" Mary paused to think of the word as she, too, looked at Clarissa. "I want to say caring, but it's more than that. It's almost feral, how protective I feel towards Clarissa and Mikey."

Bradley chuckled softly. "The she-lion defending her cubs," he whispered.

"Exactly," Mary said. "Don't mess with my cubs. I've never been a violent person…"

Bradley's cough interrupted her, and she immediately turned to him. "What?" she asked.

"I've talked to your brothers," he teased. "I've heard stories."

She shrugged and grinned. "Well, mostly, that was self-defense."

"Mostly?" he asked.

"Well, Tom's nose was a misunderstanding," she admitted.

"A misunderstanding?" Bradley questioned.

"Yes, he misunderstood that I was not in the mood to be teased," she replied. "But, I quickly cleared up that misconception."

"With your fist," he said.

"I was thirteen," she said. "It was hormones."

"I heard it was an amazing right cross," he replied.

"My fist hurt for a week," she said. "And it wasn't broken, just bruised."

"Badly," Bradley inserted. "But his pride was probably more injured than his nose."

"I never told anyone," she said immediately.

He glanced down at her. "Really? See, even at thirteen you were considerate and kind," he replied, kissing the top of her head again.

"Yep, and it only cost him half of his allowance for six weeks," she added with a smile.

Bradley choked back his laughter so he wouldn't wake up Clarissa.

"Shhhhhh," she whispered, her eyes filled with mirth.

He slid his arm from around her shoulders and cupped her face in his hands. "I am so glad you are on my side," he said tenderly. "I love you."

"I love you, too," she murmured just before his lips covered hers in a tender tribute.

"Do you guys ever stop smooching?" Mike teased as he appeared in Clarissa's room.

They slowly broke apart and turned to Mike. "Not if I can help it," Bradley said. "How'd it go with Ian?"

"He's on his way," Mike said. "He should be here in a couple of hours."

Bradley stood up and helped Mary to her feet. "I'll sleep downstairs on the couch and wait for him," he offered.

"But I could…" Mary began.

"You and Mikey need to get some sleep," Bradley insisted. "Besides, I have very fond memories of sleeping on that couch. Go to bed."

He bent down and kissed her again. She smiled at him and then turned to Mike. "Thank you," she said earnestly. "We wouldn't survive without you."

Mike smiled at her. "And don't you forget that," he teased. "Now, go to bed."

Shaking her head, she smiled. "So many bossy men in my life," she muttered. "Good night."

Once the door to Clarissa's bedroom closed, Bradley's face sobered. "Okay, what's really going on here?"

Chapter Seven

Rosie yawned widely as she made her way from her bedroom, with her pillow and an extra blanket, to the couch in the living room. She glanced up at the clock on the wall, midnight. She sighed, as much as she loved Stanley, sometimes his snoring had her beating a quick retreat to the couch before, in her sleep-deprived state, she decided to hit him over the head with her pillow. She put her pillow at one end of the couch and the shook the blanket out so it covered the rest of the couch.

She was about to climb under the covers when she saw something move out of the corner of her eye. She turned quickly and looked around the room. Everything seemed to be in place. The electric fireplace was glowing softly, and the Christmas tree was still lit, both casting soft light into the room.

Shaking her head, she placed her hands on her hips and studied the room again. She was sure she saw a shadow. Then she smiled. *Of course*, she thought, *there must be a smear on my glasses.* She reached up and realized she had left her glasses on the nightstand next to the bed. Shrugging, she turned back to the couch and saw it again, a shadow along the wall next to the Christmas tree.

Walking over to the tree, she moved the gifts she'd already placed under it. Nothing was back there. She checked the curtains on the same wall, but there was nothing there either. She studied the wall and wondered if a passing car could have reflected off something in the house and caused the shadow.

"That's probably it," she said to herself. "Just a reflection from a car." She shook her head. "I've just been spending too much time thinking about ghosts," she decided with a firm nod. "Nothing paranormal about it at all."

She sat down on the couch and slipped under the covers, turning so her back was facing the room. In a few minutes, sounds of Rosie's much softer snoring were harmonizing with Stanley's deeper ones. The shadow slipped out from behind the tree and glided to look down on the sleeping woman.

An eerie giggle whispered throughout the room, but Rosie continued to sleep.

"I get my way," the shadow whispered. "I always get my way, sooner or later."

He looked down at Rosie again. "But tonight, you're too close. You'd smell the fire too quickly. It wouldn't be as much fun."

He slowly glided away from her towards the tree. "But don't worry," he promised. "I'll be back."

Chapter Eight

"What did she tell you?" Mike asked Bradley once he heard the door to the master bedroom open and close.

"Nothing," Bradley said. "I didn't want to bring it up while we were watching Clarissa."

"Okay, let's go out into the hall," Mike suggested. "I'll still be able to watch over Clarissa from there."

They quietly made their way into the hall. "Earlier tonight, when everyone was still here, Mary saw something in the kitchen when she was getting her glass of milk," Mike explained. "Some kind of shadow in the corner of the room. I came in as she was checking things out, and she kind of brushed it off."

Mike sighed and floated away a few steps, then he turned to Bradley. "I have to admit that ever since our experience in the asylum, when Mary was lured away from us, I've been on edge," he said.

"Because something was able to get into her mind," Bradley said, "and trick her into leaving the safety of the group."

Mike nodded. "Yeah, that's powerful," he said. "And when something can pull you along like that..." He paused for a moment and then met Bradley's eyes.

"Tonight, it said it wanted Mary," he said, the concern evident in his face. "And in the asylum, it called out for her. How did she get on its radar? How did it even know Mary O'Reilly existed?"

"We've never had a spirit know about Mary before she actually had an initial contact with them, right?" Bradley asked.

"Yes," Mike said, nodding. "Or they were guided or attracted to her because of what she could do. But, they didn't know about her until they were in her actual presence."

"And somehow this spirit, whatever it is, was able to know about her from a distance," Bradley said. "Like a psychic connection."

"Yeah, and how much power does it have?" Mike asked. "Could it get into her mind and make her think someone needs her?"

"Could it get her to leave the house in the middle of the night?" Bradley asked, understanding Mike's fear as his own grew. "Walk somewhere, drive somewhere..."

"Exactly," Mike said. "Could Clarissa be calling for her, instead of you?"

Bradley ran his hand through his hair. "Okay, this is a lot riskier than I realized," he said. "We can't leave her alone."

"Yeah, that's a good first step," he said. "But how realistic is it?"

"It's going to be damn realistic until this thing is gone," Bradley said.

"And what if we never get rid of it?" Mike asked.

"That's not an option," Bradley said. He paced up and down the hallway, then stopped and stared at Mike. "Why the hell is she not as freaked out as we are?"

"Because she hasn't thought about all of the implications yet," Mike said. "Because when she was frightened and called, I was able to chase it away. She thinks we're winning."

"And we're not?" Bradley asked.

Mike shook his head slowly. "I think we're being played," he said. "And until we know what and who we're dealing with, we're not in charge."

"Ian?" Bradley asked.

"If anyone, Ian," Mike said. "He can see it and can hear it, too. And he can research things we don't have access to."

"Like what?" Bradley asked.

"Like which one of the residents of the asylum fits with this spirit," Mike said. "And what happened to him to put him in there?"

Bradley shook his head. "This doesn't make sense," he said. "If he was in the asylum, he was mentally disabled, so we should be able..." He paused, searching for the words.

"Just because someone's crazy does not mean they aren't intelligent," Mike said. "There's a quote about how there's a fine line between genius and madness. Intelligence and personality do not die with the body. They continue with the spirit."

Bradley glanced over to his closed bedroom door and then down at his watch. "How long until Ian gets here?" he asked.

"Not soon enough," Mike replied. "Not soon enough."

Chapter Nine

Mary knew she was dreaming. Her movements were too light, too easy, and for once in a long while, she didn't have the constant urge to go to the bathroom. She looked around her surroundings in a nice house, but definitely not her house. The carpet underneath her bare feet was lush and soft. The temperature inside the house was comfortable, and there was just enough light being shed by the nightlights positioned near floor level that she could easily see where she was going.

I'm lucid dreaming, she thought easily as she walked down the hallway. *That's what Ian called it, a lucid dream. This is pretty cool. Usually in my dreams I'm—*

She froze, a startled look on her face as she looked down at her body. A sigh of relief escaped her lips when she confirmed that she was, indeed, clothed.

"Lucid dreaming or not," she muttered. "I don't want to be walking around naked in someone else's home."

She continued past the closed doors of what she assumed were bedrooms and walked to the top of the stairs. The carpeted stairs emptied onto a front hall. She stepped down to the first step and was surprised to hear the front door open and the close. Peering over the rail, she saw that the hallway was empty. "Someone must have gone outside," Mary reasoned.

Continuing down the stairs, her nose was assaulted by the acrid scent of something burning. Hurrying down the next few steps, she gasped when she saw a Christmas tree in the corner of the living room on fire. The flames were rapidly spreading to the curtains and furniture. "The family!" she cried out, hurrying back up the stairs to the hallway.

She ran to the first room, but the door was locked. She tried pounding on the door, but her hands went through the wood as if she were a ghost. She tried screaming, but her voice caught in her throat. She ran up the hall to the next door, but, once again, her hands went through to the other side of the door.

Turning back, she saw the flames leaping across the hall to the staircase and black smoke billowing up towards her. She ran back to the first room and decided to try and ram the door. She turned her shoulder towards the door. She sprinted and nearly stumbled when she slipped through the door. Looking around the room, she realized it was a little girl's room, all pink and flowery. Then she saw the bunk beds and a child asleep in each one. She tried to scream, but her voice wouldn't work. She rushed over and began slapping and pulling on the mattresses and blankets, but her efforts did nothing.

Her hands slipped through any solid material. All she could do was watch.

She turned. The black smoke had now slipped underneath the door and was slowly filling the room, layer by layer. "No!" she screamed in her mind. "No, someone needs to save them!"

"Mike," she thought desperately. "Mike! Come help me! Come save them!"

She ran to the window. The sun was just beginning to rise, reflecting pink on the snow-covered ground. She tried to break the window, but once again, she was just a shadow, her movements ineffectual.

She tried to think clearly. *Lucid dreaming*, she thought suddenly. *I can change my circumstances!*

Suddenly, I have an ax in my hands, she said in her mind, but no ax appeared.

Suddenly, the window opened, she tried, but the window remained shut.

"What the hell is going on here?" she screamed.

Her eyes were drawn to a movement outside the house. She looked out the window to see a young boy looking up at her and smiling. Suddenly, she could hear his voice inside her mind. "Mary," he called. "Welcome to my home."

"Call the fire department!" she silently screamed back as the smoke filled the room. "Save their lives."

His smiled widened, and he slowly shook his head. "No," he said simply. "No, they really have to die."

"Who are you?" the thought came unbidden as she stared at the unrepentant child through the fog that now surrounded her.

"Soon you'll find out."

Mary opened her eyes, gasping for air and struggling to wake up. The boy's voice was still echoing in her mind. Finally awake, she lay in the darkness looking up at her pristine ceiling and taking deep, calming breaths. "It was only a dream," she whispered, gratified that she could hear her voice. "Only a really bad, incredibly scary, and horrifyingly disturbing dream."

Then she huffed in frustration. "And now I have to go to the bathroom."

Sliding out of the bed, she glanced at the clock. It was midnight. "The witching hour," she said softly, grateful to hear her own voice. "Oh, wait, now the witching hour's three, right?

With a shrug, she padded across the room, pausing for a moment to look out the window to the snow-covered lawn just to be sure no one was standing in front of the house. "Really disturbing," she whispered.

Once she was finished in the bathroom, she opened her bedroom door and tiptoed to the staircase. She sniffed the air, testing for any sign of burning in the air. Not satisfied with only sniffing the second floor, she stealthily made her way down the steps, leaning heavily against the banister to keep the stairs from creaking. Once on the first floor, she quietly sniffed again and breathed a sigh of relief. No smoke.

Glancing across the room, she saw Bradley laying on the couch, and her heart filled with gratitude. The couch was about six inches too short for his body, so his feet hung out over the end. The blanket he'd used was now halfway off him, and his arm was thrown over the back of the couch for balance.

"Poor baby," she whispered as she crept across the room, picked up the blanket and gently placed it back over him. She was tempted to place a kiss on his forehead, but she was sure that would wake him up.

Stepping away from the couch, she watched him for another moment, love shining from her eyes, and then turned to go back upstairs.

As she turned, she thought she caught a glimpse of something in the kitchen. Her heart jumped, and she froze in place, staring into the darkness, willing whatever it was to show itself again. She waited and watched for several minutes, but nothing else happened. Her heart was still hammering, and her body was tense.

Strangely, she thought she smelled the scent of pine in the air. It was a comforting smell. She leaned forward and sniffed. Pine and something else...vanilla? She sniffed again and nodded. Vanilla.

Instantly, a feeling of well-being washed over her, and she smiled as the tension left her body. She yawned widely, and her eyelids suddenly felt heavy. She took a deep breath. The scent filled her lungs, and relaxed her even further. Unbidden, she turned and made her way up the stairs to her bed.

When she had reached the second floor, the shadowed figure stepped out of the kitchen and glided into the living room. He glanced over at Bradley and then raised his head to listen to the sound of the bedroom door closing. With a satisfied nod, he disappeared into the night.

Chapter Ten

When Mary awoke the next morning, the sun was shining through the window, and her bedroom was awash with bright light. She looked over to the clock on the nightstand and gasped. It was nearly nine o'clock. She rolled out of bed, grabbed her robe and started to hurry towards the door when she thought better of it and headed to the bathroom first.

A few minutes later, as she came down the stairs, she could hear voices coming from the kitchen, and she hurried to join them.

"Well, good morning, darling," Ian said, standing up from his chair and giving Mary a hug and a kiss on the cheek. "Don't you look as bright as a sunbeam."

She hugged him back. "I'm so sorry I slept in so late," she apologized, mortified. "I set my alarm for six, and I slept right through it."

"Aye, and it's a great sluggard you are," Ian teased. "Working a full-time job, preparing for the holidays, and eight months pregnant on top of that. I canna understand how Bradley puts up with you."

Bradley chuckled and walked around the table. "Don't feel bad," he said. "Ian knocked on the door last night, and I slept right through it."

"Are you serious?" Mary asked, astonished.

"Aye," Ian laughed. "Mike had to come down and open the door for me. All I got from the police chief here were snores loud enough to wake the dead."

She shook her head. "I can't believe that we both slept so soundly, considering."

Ian pulled out a chair and guided Mary to it. "And it's the considering that we need to speak about," he said seriously. "But first, how about a wee bit of porridge to get your day going?"

"Porridge?" she asked, her nose wrinkling slightly.

Ian grinned. "Clarissa licked her bowl clean," he said.

"Oh! Clarissa!" Mary exclaimed, looking around the room. "Was she late for school?"

"Are you kidding?" Mike asked. "With the greatest guardian angel on the planet taking care of her? Assisted by his lordship, the Earl of Oatmeal, we had her dressed, fed, laughing and out the door in plenty of time to catch the bus."

"You are both amazing," she said and then turned to Ian. "I would love some porridge."

A few moments later, Ian placed a bowl down in front of her. She looked down and shook her head.

"Wait, this is not porridge," she said, scooping up a minuscule spoonful and trying it. Her eyes widened as she chewed. "This is so not porridge. What did you do to it?"

Ian smiled at her. "A wee bit of cinnamon, a wee bit of cocoa, and some strawberry preserves mixed in for sweetness," he said. "That's all."

Mary took another bite. "No wonder Clarissa licked her bowl clean," she said. "I'm never going to be able to make plain oatmeal again."

He sat down next to her and smiled. "Well, now I'm flattered," he said.

"Yeah, well, before you let it go to your head," Mike said, "we should be talking about what happened last night."

Mary dropped her spoon loudly in her bowl and, with a look of astonishment, looked at the others sitting at the table. "Oh my goodness, I nearly forgot," she said. "Last night."

"What?" Bradley asked.

"I had a really bad dream," she began. "And we need to talk about that, but later. So, after the dream, I came downstairs just to check on everything because I was a little freaked out. Everything seemed fine. Bradley's blanket had slipped off, so I went over and put it back on him. Then, when I turned, I thought I saw another shadow in the kitchen."

"Why didn't you wake me?" Bradley asked.

"I don't know," Mary said. "I guess I wanted to be sure it really was a shadow and not just a reaction from the dream. I stood in the same spot and watched, but nothing happened." Then she stopped and thought about it for a moment.

"Something did happen," Ian suggested.

She slowly nodded. "Now that I think about it," she said, "I remembered smelling the scent of pine and vanilla."

"Pine and vanilla?" Mike asked.

"And it was comforting," she continued. "Like suddenly all the tension from the dream just slipped away. My whole body relaxed, and I was standing in the middle of the room yawning."

She looked at each of the men. "I don't really even remember making it back up to bed," she admitted. "I was just, like, floating in relaxation."

Ian nodded. "Which could also explain your sleeping in and Bradley's non-responsiveness when I knocked on the door," he said.

"Were we drugged?" she asked.

"I don't know," Ian said.

"Was the shadow the same size as the one you saw earlier?" Mike asked.

Mary took a deep breath and thought about his question. "No," she finally said. "No. I don't think so. I think this one was bigger, more a man's size than a child."

"And the feeling you had?" Ian asked. "Did you feel panicked? Like someone was forcing you to relax when you didn't want to?"

She shook her head. "No, it was lovely," she said. "It was like I was a child again, safe and protected. It wasn't frightening at all."

Ian turned to Bradley. "Did you dream last night?" he asked.

"Now that you mention it," Bradley replied, "I did. I remember I finished the dream just before I woke up."

"What did you dream about?" Ian asked.

"Christmas," Bradley replied. "I dreamt about Christmas."

Chapter Eleven

"I dreamt about Christmas, too," Mary added. "But it was more like a nightmare than a dream."

"What happened?" Bradley asked.

"It was a lucid dream," she turned to Ian and smiled. "And thank you for giving me that bit of knowledge. It was weird because as I was dreaming, I was aware that I was dreaming. I was saying to myself, 'Oh, that's right. Ian told me about this. I'm lucid dreaming.'"

"Good job, professor," Mike teased.

"I've a brilliant student, that's all," Ian replied.

"So, I was walking down the second-floor hallway in a house," she said. "A house I've never been in before. I walked to the staircase, and I heard the front door open and close. Then I smelled smoke. I went down a couple of steps and saw that a Christmas tree was on fire and spreading throughout the house."

"Was there anyone else downstairs?" Ian asked.

She shook her head. "No, actually, I thought about that in my dream. But there was no one there, so the sound of the door must have been someone leaving," she replied. "Then I went upstairs and tried to pound on the doors, but my hands just slipped through the wood like I was a spirit."

Ian started to speak and then shook his head. "Go on," he said.

"Okay, so then I tried shouting, but my voice didn't work," she said. "And then I tried ramming the door, but instead, I slipped through the door into the bedroom. It was a room with two little girls, and it was filling with smoke. I tried to open the window, but I couldn't. Then, because I was lucid dreaming, I tried to conjure something up. So, I told myself that I had an ax." She shook her head. "No ax."

"So, you were aware enough of the situation and of the fact that you were dreaming that you were manipulating your dream, but it wasn't working?" Ian asked.

Mary nodded. "Exactly," she said. "Then I was drawn to the window, and there was a boy standing outside looking up at me. I could hear his voice in my mind, and he wasn't going to go for help. He was watching the fire. He was enjoying the fire."

"He set the fire," Mike said.

Mary's eyes widened. "Oh my gosh, you're right," she said. "He's the one who walked out the door, just before I saw the fire."

"Do you remember what he said to you?" Ian asked.

She turned to him, astonishment on her face. "He knew my name," she said slowly. "He called me Mary. And he welcomed me to his home."

"Okay, that was a Twilight Zone experience," Mike said. Then he turned to Ian. "So, professor, what do you think?"

"I think I'm glad you came for me," he said, his voice low. "Because I think this is something more dangerous than we've ever dealt with before."

Chapter Twelve

Rosie woke up stiff and sore from a night of sleeping on the couch. She slowly sat up and tried to do some of the stretching exercises she'd learned years ago in a short-lived yoga encounter. She moaned softly as she stretched her sore arm muscles.

"Rosie, what're you caterwauling about?" Stanley asked, still buttoning his shirt as he walked into the living room from the hall. He looked at his bride and shook his head. "We got a perfectly good bed in our bedroom. Why are you sleeping on the couch?"

Rosie took a deep breath to control the immediate, angry response and calmly looked at him. "Well, if you must know," she said, "your snoring kept me up, and I finally had to come into the living room to fall asleep."

Shaking his head, Stanley shrugged. "I didn't hear nothing," he said.

"That doesn't mean you weren't snoring," Rosie insisted. "You just slept through it."

Scratching the back of his head, he looked a little confused. "Couldn't have been that loud iffen I could sleep right through it," he said.

"Oh!" Rosie huffed. "Of all the ignorant…" She placed her hands on her hips and glared at him. "Do you think I'm lying to you? Do you think I don't know loud snoring when I hear it? Do you think I would sleep out here on this lumpy couch with creepy shadows darting around the room—"

"Creepy shadows?" Stanley interrupted her. "Creepy shadows? What are you talking about?"

"Oh, you heard that did you?" Rosie said, rolling her eyes and storming past him towards the bedroom. "Well, perhaps you and the creepy shadows can make your own breakfast."

The door slammed loudly behind her.

"I heard that, too," he muttered softly, looking over his shoulder towards the door. "Iffen a woman ain't upset about one thing, she's upset about something else."

Shaking his head, he finished buttoning his shirt and walked across the room into the kitchen. "I'm just fine with making my own breakfast," he muttered softly. "I was making my breakfast fer years afore you moved in."

He opened the refrigerator door, looked inside and weighed his options. There was a bowl of leftover spaghetti and meatballs, a pie plate with a large slice of a peach pie, some vegetables to make a salad, and eggs and bacon. He pulled out the bowl of spaghetti and meatballs, scooped a generous serving onto a plate and popped it into the microwave. Then he pulled out the pie slice, put it on a smaller plate and sprayed whipped cream over the top of it. He put a placemat down at the table, put a napkin and silverware down on it and then placed a glass of ice cold milk alongside it. When the microwave beeped, he pulled out the steaming plate of pasta and set it on the placemat.

"Well, that's a well-balanced meal iffen I ever saw one," he said with a triumphant smile.

He sat down at the table and mixed the spaghetti with his fork to evenly distribute the sauce.

"Stanley," Rosie called out from the room. "You had better remember what your doctor said about your diet."

A frown appeared on his face. "Them doctors don't know what they're talking about," he grumbled. "I'm as healthy as a horse."

He looked down at the meal before him, slipped the spaghetti plate to the side and dug into the peach pie with relish. He devoured the pie and whipped cream and scraped the plate clean with his fork, just as Rosie opened the door to their bedroom. Glancing around frantically, his eyes landed on the folded newspaper at the end of the table. Quickly, he slid the dessert plate inside the pages of the paper and then pulled the spaghetti plate in front of him, twirling a bite of spaghetti onto his fork.

"What are you eating?" Rosie asked, now fully dressed.

"Spaghetti and meatballs," Stanley said, his eyes wide with innocence. "Healthy as the day is long."

She smiled at him. "I'm proud of you, Stanley," she said. "I thought for sure you would be eating peach pie for breakfast."

"Well, I ain't, as you can see fer yourself," he replied, feeling a little guilty about lying to her.

She started to walk towards the refrigerator when he jumped up and waylaid her. "I want to apologize for the snoring," he said. "Why don't you let me make you breakfast."

"Why Stanley, that's so sweet," Rosie said. "But I couldn't let you..."

"No. No. I insist," he replied, pulling out a chair for her. "Now what would you like?"

She studied him for a moment and noticed that his shirt seemed to have flakes of crust on it. Her eyes narrowed, and she glanced around the table noting the large bump in the middle of the newspaper. Then she turned back to Stanley. "Well, since you're being so generous," she said, "why don't we both split that last piece of pie. I think that would be considered moderation, don't you?"

"Split the piece of pie?" Stanley choked, feeling like his last bite was caught in his throat.

She smiled widely and nodded. "Yes, that sounds just perfect to me," she said. "Peach pie."

He looked panicked, and he searched around the room, desperate to come up with something to stay out of trouble. His eyes landed on the phone, and he took a deep breath and smiled.

"Sure. Sure, we can have pie," he said. "Mary can wait."

Rosie shook her head. "Mary? What's going on with Mary?" she asked.

"Well, never you mind," he said. "Breakfast is more important. A phone call to Mary can wait."

"She wanted me to call her?" Rosie asked, suspicious of Stanley's motives.

He nodded his head. "Yeah, she said she wanted you to tell her about the shadowy thing you saw last night."

Rosie picked up the phone and stared at Stanley for a long moment. "I'm going to call Mary, and if she doesn't know what I'm talking about, so help me Stanley…"

"Just call her and find out," he replied.

Watching him, she dialed the phone. "Hello Mary, this is Rosie," she said. "Stanley was just saying I should call you about the shadows I saw darting around the living room last night."

Her eyes widened, and her jaw dropped. "Why, of course we can," she said, staring at Stanley. "Yes, we'll be right over."

She hung up the phone and shook her head. "Well, I'm sorry I ever doubted you," she said. "Can you forgive me?"

"'Course I can," Stanley said, picking up his plate and walking it across the room. "I'll just stick my plate in the refrigerator, and we can go right now."

"Yes," Rosie agreed. "She seemed a little anxious."

"Well, it's probably nothing," he assured her, helping her with her coat. "But we shouldn't let her worry, you know, considering her condition."

"You're right. It's probably nothing," Rosie agreed, but her voice didn't quite convince either of them.

Chapter Thirteen

Mary hung up the phone and slowly laid it down on the table. "That was Rosie," she said, her voice heavy with concern. "She said that she saw a shadowy figure in her house last night."

"When?" Bradley asked.

"I didn't ask," Mary replied regretfully. "I was so worried I just asked them to come over here right away."

"Do you think it was the same spirit that visited you?" Ian asked.

"Why would he have gone to their house?" Bradley asked. "And didn't you think you saw him later when I was asleep?"

"If that was the same shadowy figure," Mary said.

"How many shadowy figures do we have in our house?" Bradley asked.

"Well, there's Ian…" Mike replied, trying to lighten the mood. Then he shook his head. "Sorry, inappropriate timing I know. But, you know, there could be more than one spirit involved."

Mary looked at him. "The last one, the one I saw when Bradley was asleep," she said. "I didn't feel as creeped out by it. I mean, if I were as creeped out, I wouldn't have gone upstairs to bed, right?"

Ian shrugged. "Well, it all depends on the entity," he explained. "If he's a spirit that can influence your thoughts and actions, he could have wanted you to feel safe and go to bed."

"Why would he do that?" Mary asked.

Bradley sat back in his chair and glanced around the table. "Because if we were all sleeping, he could set another fire," he said slowly. "And if we were sleeping hard enough that someone knocking on the door couldn't wake us…"

"It would have been like my dream," Mary said, a chill running up her back. "We would have died in our sleep."

She rested her hands on her stomach, instinctively protecting the child inside of her. "So, why didn't he do it?" she asked.

"It could have been that I interrupted his plan," Ian said. "It sounds like I arrived an hour or so after you'd gone back to bed. So, perhaps he was waiting until you were sound asleep, and by then it was too late."

"That makes sense," Bradley said. "I don't like your answer, but it makes perfect sense."

Mary looked over at Mike. "Can he do that?" she asked. "Can a spirit come into my house and set a fire? I thought there were rules."

Mike met her eyes and sighed. "This one wasn't sent to you," he said. "He didn't come needing help. He followed you from the asylum. And, really, the asylum wasn't in the plan book either. So, to answer your question, this one is beyond the rules. He writes his own rules."

She turned back to Bradley, fear in her eyes. "What do we do?"

He placed his hand over hers and gave it a comforting squeeze. "Well, first, we don't panic," he said. "We have more power on our team than he does."

"How do you know?" she asked.

"We pushed him back at the asylum, and Mike pushed him out last night," he said. "It sounds like he prefers to lurk in the shadows and cause problems when no one is watching." He turned to Mike and Ian. "So, we watch."

"I like that plan," Ian agreed. "But we're also going to need to find out who he is and why he's here if we are ever going to get rid of him."

"So, we divide and conquer," Mary said.

"Wait a minute," Bradley said. "I don't like the sound…"

"We both can't go this time," Mary said, interrupting him. "We can't leave Clarissa here without one of us here. Mike is powerful, but…"

"But sometimes my hands are tied," Mike admitted.

"And we can't send Clarissa over to Brennan's, because he could follow her," Mary continued. "We can't risk their family, too."

"Mary and I can go back up to the asylum," Ian said. "We can look for records there and in the nearby town."

"We can also find out if the house fire was local," Mary said. "Small towns remember things like that."

"You won't take any risks?" Bradley said.

"I promise," she replied, meeting his eyes. "I will do nothing that will put me or Mikey in danger."

"Aye, and she wouldna have a choice, anyway," Ian replied. "I wouldna allow it."

Bradley ran his hand through his hair and nodded. "Okay, I have a friend who has a vacation house up there," he said. "I'll call him and ask if I can use it."

"We can just stay in a hotel," Mary said.

Bradley shook his head. "There are too many places to start a fire in a hotel," he said. "This place is easier to protect."

"Good point," Ian said, turning and smiling at Mary. "I guess we get to be roommates again."

"Thank you," she replied.

"For what?" he asked.

"For dropping everything and coming to help," she said. "For interrupting your life."

His smile faltered slightly. "Ah, well, I was looking for a wee distraction just now," he said softly. "And this seems to fit the bill."

He turned to Bradley. "The fellow you borrowed the ghost hunting equipment from," he said. "Wyatt, right? Wyatt Hermann?"

Bradley nodded. "Yes, why?"

"Do you think he'd mind if we borrowed it again?" Ian asked. "It'd be helpful to have some sensors around the house to tell us if we've got company."

"Good idea," Mary said as she pushed herself to her feet. "Okay, I'll go upstairs and pack."

"Packing's gotta wait," Mike said. "Rosie and Stanley are here."

Ian stood up and shook his head. "You go on up," he said. "I'll talk with them. Then we can leave as soon as possible."

Chapter Fourteen

"Ian!" Rosie exclaimed when he opened the door for them. "I had no idea you would be here."

Ian leaned forward and kissed Rosie's cheek. "Well, darling," he said, "I just couldn't keep myself away from you." Then he winked at her. "And your cooking."

She smiled back. "I made a peach pie yesterday…" she began.

"I ate it all," Stanley inserted quickly, frowning at Ian. "Every last bite."

Rosie turned and stared at him. "You did what?"

Realizing what he'd just said, Stanley shook his head and began to stammer. "Er, um, what I meant to say," he began, clearly faltering for a viable explanation. In desperation, he sent a look of pure despair to Ian.

"Ah, well, I hate to disrupt this discussion," Ian inserted, "but we really have a serious situation on our hands."

Rosie turned back to Ian. "What do you mean?" she asked.

"Last night, a shadowy figure tried to harm Mary," Ian said.

"Oh, no!" Rosie exclaimed, hurrying into the house. "She didn't say anything over the phone. Is she okay?"

Stanley walked in behind her, and Ian closed the door. "Aye, she's fine," Ian said. "Mike was able to help her. But they felt the situation was serious enough to call me."

"A shadowy figure," Stanley said, forgetting his earlier distress. "Like the one Rosie said she saw?"

Ian nodded slowly. "Exactly right," he said. "And that's why Mary was so insistent you both come by."

"Well, she was goldurn right to ask us to come over," Stanley exclaimed. "And, iffen you don't mind me saying so, she probably should have called us last night when she called you. We're part of the team, too."

Ian studied Stanley for a long moment. He could see the disappointment in the older man's eyes, see the pride in his stance and the courage in the slight lift of his chin. This was a man who would sacrifice for the people he loved, and a man who had proven that he was someone you could rely on.

"You're right, Stanley," Ian said earnestly. "We should have called you and kept you in the loop. You are a vital part of the team."

The look of disappointment disappeared from Stanley's eyes, and he smiled. "Well, I'm here now," he said with a shrug. "That's all that matters."

"Yes, that's right," Ian replied. "Why don't we sit at the table. I can explain what's going on here, and then you can tell me about what happened last night."

They sat at the table, and Ian gave them an overview of what had happened to Mary the night before, including her dream.

"Well, how odd," Rosie replied. "Because it was about the same time Mary came downstairs the second time that I was in the living room." She shot a quick glance at Stanley and then turned back to Ian. "I was having trouble sleeping."

"What did you see?" Ian asked.

"Well, I actually saw it several times," she explained. "A shadow on the wall near the Christmas tree. At first I thought it was my imagination, but then I saw it again. Then I thought it might be a smear on my glasses, but it wasn't. Finally, I saw it again, and I walked over to the Christmas tree and took the packages away from it, to see if some cat or something had gotten into the house."

"But you didn't find anything?" Ian asked.

She shook her head. "No, nothing at all," she said. "So, I went to bed."

"Back in your bedroom?" Ian asked.

"No," she said. "I was feeling restless, so I slept on the couch."

"She's just being nice," Stanley interrupted. "I was snoring loud enough to wake the dead. Poor Rosie couldn't sleep next to me, so she went into the living room."

"How did you feel?" Ian asked.

"Angry as all get out," Rosie replied. "He sounded like a freight train running through the middle of the bed."

Ian smiled and bit back a chuckle. "No, I mean when you saw the shadow," he explained. "How did you feel?"

She thought about it for a moment. "It made my skin crawl," she finally said. "As a matter of fact, when I finally laid down, I turned away from the room and covered up as much as I could. I felt a little foolish, but it made me feel safer."

"Not foolish at all," Ian said. "That was your primal instinct guiding you. Your subconscious felt there was danger, and you instinctively sheltered yourself."

"Oh, well, that does make me feel a little better," she replied. "So, the shadowy figure, is it dangerous?"

"We think so," Ian said. "But we don't know. And, because there was a shadowy figure here at the same time, we can't be quite sure the same one was at your house."

"How many goldurn shadowy figures are running around?" Stanley asked.

"I wish I could tell you, Stanley," Ian said. "But I will tell you that if Rosie felt her skin crawl, I would definitely take that as a sign that it could be dangerous."

"So, how do I protect Rosie?" Stanley asked.

"Right now, we're working on a theory that the spirit we're dealing with is the boy from Mary's dream."

"The one that set fire to the house?" Rosie asked.

"Yes," Ian replied. "And we're going up to Wisconsin to revisit the asylum and see if we can learn anything more about the boy."

"And in the meantime, I'll sleep on the couch," Stanley said. "Iffen you're right and my snoring can wake the dead, maybe it can scare 'em away, too."

"Just make sure your fire alarms are in working order," Ian said. "And be careful. We'll let you know as soon as we find something out."

Chapter Fifteen

About an hour later, Bradley entered the house carrying a large cardboard box filled with electronic equipment. "Wyatt let me borrow everything he had," he said, walking through the living room and placing the box on the table.

Then he put his hand in his jacket pocket and pulled out a piece of paper and a set of keys. "And here are the directions and the keys to the summer house."

Mary peeked over the top of the box. "We should leave some of this here, for you and for Rosie and Stanley," Mary suggested. "What do you think, Ian?"

Ian glanced over at Bradley. "How big is this summer house?" he asked.

"I've never been in it," Bradley said. "But it sounds more like a cottage than a house. A couple of bedrooms, a living room, a kitchen and a bathroom. I don't think there's even a basement."

"Everything on one floor?" Ian asked.

Bradley nodded. "Yeah, there's only one floor."

Ian picked up the various monitors. "With my equipment and a couple of these, we will be more than protected," he said. "And, even though you have Mike, I think it wouldn't hurt for you to have a couple of them on stand-by."

"How about Rosie and Stanley?" Bradley asked.

"I think they need some too," Ian said. "Whatever visited them last night was not friendly."

"Okay, take what you need, and I'll distribute the rest," Bradley said. Then he turned to Mary. "Do you have everything you need?"

She smiled and nodded. "Yes, my suitcase is upstairs," she said. "I packed for a week, but I don't think we'll be up there that long."

He paused for a moment. "So, did you actually pack for a couple of days, but you have enough clothes for a week?" he teased. "Or did you pack for a week and have enough clothes for a month?"

Her smile turned to a grin, and she shrugged. "It's always wise to be prepared," she said.

Turning to Ian, Bradley shook his head. "I hope you brought your large SUV," he said. "Or, I could hook up a trailer to your car."

"It canna be that bad," Ian replied, looking a little worried.

"Oh, yes, it can," Bradley said.

Laughing, Mary shook her head. "No, it's not," she said. "I only have one suitcase filled with clothes and one tote filled with toiletries."

"Toiletries?" Ian said. "A tote filled with toiletries?"

Bradley nodded. "That's what I said the first time we traveled together," he said. "Body wash, deodorant, shampoo and razor blades. One quart-sized Ziploc™ and we're good, right?"

"Aye," Ian said. "And I tend to use the body wash as shampoo." He looked at Mary. "What could you possibly have in a tote?"

She shook her head. "You wouldn't understand it, even if I explained it," she said. "I tried with Bradley, and it was totally incomprehensible to him."

"They have hair products," Bradley said. "They don't just shampoo. They have to condition, and then they have to oil, gloss, smooth, wax and spray. Or something like that."

"Sounds like a car wash," Ian said.

"That's what I said," Bradley said. "Before she threw something at me."

"It was a pillow," Mary replied. "And you deserved it."

"And I won't even go into everything they put on their faces in the morning, after washing, toning, moisturizing and priming," Bradley added.

"Priming?" Ian said, looking from Bradley to Mary. "Priming?"

"You will never understand what we do to make ourselves beautiful for you," Mary replied.

"See, that's the thing," Bradley said, putting his arm around her shoulders. "I see her first thing in the morning, without all that stuff, and she is already the most beautiful woman in the world."

She smiled up at him. "Okay, that was nice," she said. "And you are totally out of the dog house for saying all of that other stuff. Now, come on upstairs and help me carry my stuff down."

Bradley chuckled. "We'll be down in a minute," he said to Ian.

"Take your time," he said. "I'll load up the things from Wyatt and then rearrange the back of the SUV so I can fit Mary's things."

"Very funny," Mary said as she walked up the stairs to the sound of Ian's chuckles.

Once she and Bradley were in the bedroom, she closed the door and turned to him, her arms folded over her chest. "I'll be fine," she said softly.

He sighed and put down the suitcase he'd just lifted. "I was that obvious?" he asked.

She walked across the room and wrapped her arms around his waist and leaned against his tall, sturdy frame. "I understand locker room banter," she said. "You talk about inconsequential things so you're not thinking about what's out there on the street waiting for you."

He hugged her, and laid his cheek against the top of her head. "It's killing me to let you leave," he whispered. "Not knowing what you're facing. Not being there for you."

She nodded, her cheek pressed against his chest. "I know," she said. "But I'll be careful. I won't take any risks."

"Ian won't let you take any risks," he muttered.

She laughed softly. "There's that too," she agreed. "And I won't endanger my life or Mikey's life." She looked up at him. "I have way too much to live for."

"I love you, Mary," he said, his heart in his eyes.

"I love you back," she replied and then leaned up to press her lips against his. Then she stepped back and nodded. "Be safe and be careful here. As soon as we figure out what or who we're dealing with, I'll let you know."

He kissed her on her forehead and then picked up her suitcase. "Solve this case quickly," he said. "I don't like sleeping alone anymore."

She grinned. "And I don't like you sleeping alone."

Chapter Sixteen

"I don't want you sleeping alone in the living room," Stanley argued. "I'm the one that's snoring. I should sleep on the couch."

Rosie shook her head. "With your bad back, one night on the couch would have you doubled over in pain. I can sleep on the couch."

"I ain't having you out here facing them shadow creatures," Stanley replied.

"You ain't. I mean, you aren't," Rosie exclaimed. "I may be your wife, but that doesn't mean you get to order me around."

Stanley sighed and rubbed his forehead. "I ain't trying to order you around, Rosie," he said softly. "I'm just trying to protect you. And I gotta protect you, 'cause I love you."

Shaking her head, Rosie sat down on a chair, tears in her eyes. "Oh, Stanley, I'm sorry," she said. "I guess this whole shadowy ghost thing has me on edge."

He walked over to her and rubbed her back. "And I'm guessing you ain't had much sleep on account of my snoring, on top of everything else."

She nodded, pulling out a handkerchief and blotting her eyes. "Well, not as much as I'm used to," she admitted. "Still, that's no reason to bicker with you."

He moved over in front of her and sat on the edge of the coffee table so he could face her. He took her hands in his and met her eyes. "Ain't it funny that as folks get closer to Christmas, it seems like tempers flare up more and folks lose patience with each other? Like the spirit of good will has to battle against spirits of anger, impatience and meanness."

Rosie thought about his words for a moment. "You know, I wonder if that isn't true," she replied. "There's always a battle between good and evil. I wonder if evil ramps things up because this is such a season of good?"

"Sure sounds like a logical explanation," he said. "So, what do we do so we ain't going at it like a pair of old roosters?"

She smiled at him. "Well, I suppose we just need to recognize it for what it is," she suggested. "We need to have even more patience and understanding. We need to slow down and remember how much we love each other."

Stanley stared into her eyes for a few long moments. "I love you with all my heart, Rosie-gal," he said softly, his voice breaking. "Ain't nothing more important to me than you."

Her eyes softly misting, she smiled at him. "And I love you, Stanley," she replied. "You are the best man I've ever known."

She leaned forward and placed a kiss on his lips.

He smiled up at her. "So, I'm gonna sleep on the couch tonight," he said. "It's decided."

Her eyes widened in surprise. "It's not decided, you old coot," she replied.

His chuckle caught her off guard. "Ain't never loved being called an old coot afore," he said. "Now it's music to my ears."

"Oh, dear," she said with a sigh. "I'm afraid I reacted badly. But I want to protect you too, and I just don't want you sleeping out here in the front room with the shadow thing."

"Well, we got to figure this out so we're both happy," Stanley admitted.

He stood up and walked back to the hallway, his hands on his hips, and studied the back of his house. Then he looked over his shoulder. "Well, I could sleep in the guest room here," he said. "That's the closest one to the living room, but it ain't in the living room. Then you can sleep in the bedroom, and neither one of us has to share a room with the shadow thing."

Rosie joined him at the beginning of the hallway and slipped her hand inside of his. "That could work," she said slowly. "As long as you agree not to do anything that would put you at risk."

He lifted their clasped hands and kissed her hand. "I got too much too lose," he said, smiling into her eyes. "I ain't gonna risk nothing."

Chapter Seventeen

The gray-green Land Rover cruised across the Wisconsin border and headed north on Highway 69. Ian glanced over at Mary and nodded towards the phone she held in her hand. "Any luck?" he asked.

She nodded. "Dee had the original email from the owner of the asylum," she said. "He's not only forwarding it to me but also calling the owner and letting him know that he's asked us to do a little follow-up work for the show."

"Ahhh," Ian said with a knowing smile. "The owner is after the publicity."

"Yes," Mary said. "He wants to turn the asylum into a paranormal destination."

Ian shook his head. "Does that sound as crazy to you as it does to me?" he asked. "Paranormal destination. It's not a freaking zoo. People could get hurt. People could die…"

Mary stared at the usually laid-back Scot in surprise. She'd never heard him so adamant about something. "Ian, are you okay?" she asked.

He stopped and took a deep breath. "Aye," he said. "I'm sorry, Mary. I've no excuse for tearing off like that."

"Maybe not an excuse," she said. "But a reason. What's going on?"

"Ah, well, as much as I'd like to tell you, I cannot," he said. "It could risk a life, actually more than one life. But, this I can disclose. I'll never take the paranormal, any part of it, for granted again. There's powerful, and often dangerous, capabilities that we as humans have no inkling of."

Mary shivered and nodded. "I'm beginning to understand that myself," she said. "Beginning to understand that not all ghosts are merely lost souls who are looking for their way to the light."

He nodded. "Are you frightened?" he asked softly.

She studied him for a moment. "Just between you and me?" she asked.

He nodded.

"Then yes," she said. "Yes, I'm frightened. I felt something beyond paranormal when I spoke with that ghost, or whatever it was. Something more disturbing."

"Did you ever watch the show Fantasy Island?" Ian asked.

Mary shook her head. "Wow, talk about a change of topics," she said with a smile.

He laughed and nodded. "Well, yes and no," he said. "I watched reruns of the show for a research project."

"Are you kidding me?" she asked. "Research project? What kind of research?"

"Well actually, it was a research project regarding paranormal truths found in pop culture," he said.

"Sounds like a great project," she said.

"It was. I got to watch Buffy the Vampire Slayer, Fantasy Island, Kolchak: The Night Stalker, My Mother the Car…"

"My Mother the Car?" Mary interrupted.

"Sure," Ian replied with a grin. "It's about reincarnation. The guy's mom comes back as a car and tries to help him with his life."

"So, did you learn any great truths in your research?" she asked.

"Surprisingly, yes," he said. "Much of the information used to create the shows were from bits and pieces of legend some screenwriter dug up and then used to create a storyline. There was one in Fantasy Island where Roddy McDowell portrayed the devil."

Mary thought about it for a moment. "Okay, I can kind of see it," she said.

"What? Is it because he's Scottish?" he teased.

She laughed. "No, it's because of his narrow face," she said. "And why I think the devil has a narrow face is beyond me."

"Okay, continuing with my research," Ian said.

"Your television watching," Mary inserted.

"A woman has made a pact with the devil because her husband was in a terrible car accident and is going to die," he explained. "So, the devil says he will save her husband's life in return for her immortal soul."

"I could see that trade," she said, and when he looked surprised, she shook her head. "Not that I would do it."

"So, she comes to Fantasy Island on the anniversary of the agreement to try and get out of the contract," Ian continued. "But, since the contract was entered into of her own free will and choice, there's not much Mr. Rourke can do."

"I've got to say that Ricardo Montalban was a very good-looking man," she said.

Ian smiled. "In a very manly way, I agree," he said. "The guy was ripped. Anyway, they meet, the woman and her husband, Rourke, and Roddy the devil. And, the devil's ready to take her immortal soul when Rourke pops up with the fact that because she's pregnant, the devil isn't allowed to touch her."

"What?" Mary asked.

"Because this woman is pregnant," Ian repeated slowly, "the devil has to stay away. The innocent soul within her protected her."

Mary placed her hands on her belly. "And why are you telling me this?" she asked.

"Sometimes the truth we find in legends happens after the legends are created," he said. "Because legend becomes belief and then belief becomes truth."

"So, if I believe something strongly enough, it becomes real?" she asked.

"Books have been written about it," Ian said. "The power of positive thinking. What you believe is what shapes your destiny. If you believe you will succeed, you will. If you believe you're going to fail…"

Mary nodded. "I will fail," she finished. "So, if I believe having Mikey inside of me will protect me…"

"Then whatever is challenging you will not hold the power of fear over you," he said. "You'll know that you can defeat it. You will be strong, and you will be focused."

Mary took a deep breath and then nodded. "You know, Professor McDougal, you are fairly brilliant."

He smiled at her. "You're just saying that because you want me to make you more porridge," he said.

"Well, there is that," she laughed. "And there's just the fact that you always know what I need to hear. Thank you."

"My pleasure," he said, glancing at her for a long moment and then back at the road. "We're going to win, Mary."

With her hands on her baby bump, she nodded and smiled. "Yes. Yes, we are."

Chapter Eighteen

The small town of Flynt, Wisconsin, was located at the southern tip of Wisconsin's Driftless Region, the area of Wisconsin that was untouched by glacier movement about 10,000 years ago. Instead of the rolling farmland Ian and Mary had traveled through on most of their drive, suddenly the topography was sculpted with forested hillsides, limestone bluffs, fast-flowing trout streams that were never totally frozen over and snow-covered prairies.

"This reminds me a wee bit of home," Ian said as they drove down the winding country roads. "Although I don't think we ever had this much snow."

"Do you miss home?" Mary asked.

He glanced over and smiled. "Ah, well then, home is where the heart is, is it not?" he asked. "And for now, my heart is well-situated here in the Midwest."

"Speaking of your heart, how's Gillian?" she asked.

Ian didn't answer for several moments, but Mary could see that he was working out an answer by the tension in his jaw. "I'm sorry," she inserted. "I didn't mean to… I didn't know…"

He smiled at her. "No, it's not your fault at all," he said kindly. "It's just that Gillian and I are working on a project that requires confidentiality, so there's only so much I can share."

"Oh, I understand," she replied, but she really didn't understand how a project could be compromised by her inquiring of Gillian's well-being. "She's fine though, right?"

He nodded slowly. "Aye, I'm sure she's well," he replied. "But she's been gone for a while and I'm missing her terribly."

Reaching over, she patted his arm. "It's hard when you're in love, isn't it?" she asked. "Even a few days seems like an eternity."

He smiled, but it didn't reach his eyes. "You've the right of it there," he said. "An eternity is what it feels like."

"I'm sure she's missing you, too," Mary said.

"I'm sure she is," he replied. "I'm sure she is."

He slowed the SUV down as they came to a four-way stop and then turned left. The scenery turned from forests to residential, with driveways appearing on either side of the road. Within a few miles, they were entering the small town of Flynt.

The downtown was only a few blocks long, with red brick buildings standing side by side. On one corner, an original mercantile store had been restored and now boasted large, floor to ceiling display windows that showcased a collection of unique items. Other vintage buildings held eclectic stores and restaurants that would have had the original residents of the community scratching their heads in confusion, from frozen yogurt and cappuccinos to crystals and computers. The town's offerings seemed to reflect that tourism was the main attraction these days. At the end of Main Street, the old courthouse stood on a hill overlooking the downtown, its domed roof and stone façade standing majestically in the center of town.

"What a cute town," Mary exclaimed as they drove slowly down the street.

Ian chuckled. "Well, maybe if we solve our problem quickly, we can do a little Christmas shopping before we leave."

She turned away from the window and glanced at him. "You really shouldn't tease like that," she said. "I just might take you up on it."

"Whose teasing?" he countered. "I'll wager you there's an antique store in this town that will be filled with hidden treasures."

She studied him for a moment. "Okay, deal," she said. "We get done soon enough, we go shopping."

"So, do we start at the courthouse or at the library?" Ian asked, indicating by the turn of his head a modest, brick building on another corner of the downtown.

"Let's go to the courthouse first," she suggested. "And then the library."

They passed another nondescript building, and Mary read the small sign posted on the window as they drove by. "Oh, there's the newspaper. We could stop by there, too. They often have a morgue."

"Excuse me?" Ian asked.

"You know, a room where they keep old copies of newspapers," she said. "Don't they call that a morgue in Scotland?"

"No. Not that I've ever heard," he replied. "We only put bodies in our morgues. Well, actually, we put bodies in mortuaries, but occasionally we refer to them as morgues."

Mary shook her head. "It always amazes me that we all started off with the same language," she teased.

"Aye, I agree," Ian replied. "You took it here to the United States and completely destroyed it."

"Improved on it," she insisted.

He grinned. "Utterly and completely mutilated it," he insisted.

Chuckling, she nodded. "Agree to disagree," she said. "Truce."

He laughed. "Aye, truce."

Chapter Nineteen

Ian parked his car in the small parking lot behind the courthouse, and they used the back access door to enter the building. They followed the tiled floor to the front lobby where a security guard sat at a small table near the stairs.

"Can I help you?" he asked.

"Yes, thank you," Mary replied. "We're looking for information on the old county asylum."

He stared at them, his eyes narrowing. "You ain't one of them ghost-hunting groups are you?" he asked.

"No, we're not," Ian said.

"You're not from around here," the guard said to Ian.

Ian shook his head. "No, I'm not," he said. "I'm from Chicago." Then he smiled. "And before that, Edinburgh."

The man nodded. "Thought so. The wife likes them BBC shows."

"She has excellent taste," Ian replied. "I'm a professor from the University of Edinburgh, and I'm working with the University of Chicago on some research. We're looking for old records from the asylum to add to our data pool. Do you have any records like that here at the courthouse?"

The guard looked slowly around the totally empty room and then leaned closer to Mary and Ian. "I'll tell you what," he said. "I get the feeling the folks here at the county ain't none too proud of what happened out there at the asylum. When they finally closed it down, they didn't do nothing to bring those records back to the courthouse. They just kind of left 'em out there, hoping, you know, they'd just all go away."

"Just what happened out there?" Mary asked.

The guard looked around one more time. "Well," he said, lowering his voice, "there was the normal things you hear about when you're dealing with facilities that are overcrowded and underfunded, neglect and abuse. But then there were some strange things happened out there. Suicides, supposedly accidental deaths, and then there were those fires."

"Fires?" Ian asked.

The man nodded his head. "Spontaneous combustion is what some were calling it," he said. "But I don't know about that. Can't be too spontaneous if you can find an accelerant in the room that had the fire."

"The asylum never fully caught fire?" Ian asked, remembering that there were no signs of fire damage when they had investigated the institution weeks ago.

The guard shook his head. "No, just little fires in individual rooms," he said. "Just enough fire to get the job done."

"The job done?" Mary repeated.

"Killed 'em," the guard said. "It was either smoke or burning, but every time one of those random fires were set, somebody died." He stopped and looked around again. "Rumor was, it was some kind of beyond this world event."

"Paranormal?" Ian asked.

"Yeah, that's right," the guard said. "That's the word they used. Paranormal."

"Who used that word?" Ian asked.

"The doctor that took care of them out at the asylum," he replied.

"A medical doctor?" Mary asked.

The guard shook his head. "No, one of them shrink kind of doctors," he said. "You know, a psychiatrist. Name of Buus, Dr. Mark Buus."

"Do you think we could speak with him?" Ian asked.

"Ain't likely," the guard said.

"Why not?" Mary asked.

"He's the last one who died out there," the guard replied. "And that was the last straw. The county moved all the inmates to other facilities and then chained up the doors. They was all too spooked by half to even do much of an investigation. Didn't want to end up toast."

Mary glanced over at Ian. Did she dare ask the man about the little boy and the fire? Ian seemed to read her thoughts and slowly nodded in affirmation.

"It, um, seems that your town has a sad history with fires," Mary said, trying to keep her voice light. "When I was, um, doing research with Professor McDougal, I discovered a story about a fire on Christmas Day, some time back. I thought the entire family was killed."

The guard shook his head. "No, not the whole family," he said. "The boy. Tony. He survived."

"Tony," Mary repeated. "He survived the fire?"

The guard met her eyes. "No, he started the fire," he said, his voice filled with disgust. "Stood out there on the lawn on Christmas morning. A smile a mile wide on his face while he watched the house with his parents and sisters go up in flames."

"Why did he do it?" Mary asked.

"I was there that day," he said. "I was a rookie firefighter. I saw this kid standing out in the snow and, you know, my heart broke for him. Losing his family on Christmas Day, it had to be a terrible tragedy for him. So, as I'm checking things out, making sure no sparks spread to the garage, I see a bike with a bow on it. It's got the kid's name on it."

He took a deep breath and then wiped a little bit of perspiration from his forehead. "So, I wheel the bike over to the kid and I tell him I found it in the garage." The guard lifted his eyes and first met Mary's eyes, then turned to Ian. "The kid doesn't flinch, doesn't react emotionally at all. All he says to me is that they should have left it under the tree."

"His bike?" Mary whispered, her voice shaking. "He said he wanted his bike?"

She stepped back and leaned against the wall, her legs shaky.

"Are you okay, ma'am?" the guard asked.

She nodded, not trusting herself to speak.

"Do you remember what Tony's last name was?" Ian asked urgently.

The guard turned back to Ian. "Yeah, I'll never forget," the guard replied. "Lancaster. Tony Lancaster."

"Thank you," Ian said. "You've been very helpful. Now, I think I need to get some fresh air for my assistant."

"Yeah, pregnancy's a tough job," he replied, as he looked at Mary. "Good luck to you."

She smiled. "Thank you," she said, her voice slightly weak. "Thank you so much."

Chapter Twenty

"Are you alright?" Ian asked Mary softly as they walked back down the hall towards the exit.

She nodded slowly. "I could picture it all in my mind," she said. "The boy, Tony, standing on the lawn watching. His emotionless face when he was given the bike. It just sent terror through me." She turned to Ian. "This is what we're dealing with?"

"Well, I think we still have to do a little more research to figure it out," he said. "The fires seem more than a little coincidental."

He stopped in front of the door and opened it up for Mary. She stepped outside in the early afternoon, winter sun and took a deep, cleansing breath of the biting cold air.

"I agree," Mary finally said, feeling much less shaky. "And, now that it's not going to be a surprise, I promise you that I won't wimp out again."

Ian put his arm around her shoulders and guided her back towards the car. "You didn't wimp out," he said. "You reacted to a bit of frightening information, and I don't blame you in the least."

She shrugged. "Thanks, but I will do better."

"Okay, so where to next?" he asked. "The café for some lunch and a bathroom break?"

She stopped and looked at him. "How did you—"

"Bradley gave me some pointers on escorting a pregnant woman," Ian interrupted. "Food and facilities are top priorities."

She laughed. "Actually, food and facilities sound perfect right now," she agreed. "And then we can plan our next moves."

They drove to a small café on Main Street with a sign that boasted Door County cherry pie and the flakiest pasties in the Driftless Region.

Mary studied the sign for a moment. "Pasties?" she asked, pronouncing the word with a long a sound. "But I thought those were…"

"Pasties," Ian corrected, using the short a sound in the word. "A wonderful meat pie originally from Cornwall in the UK. It rhymes with nasty not hasty."

"Well, good, because really, it's a bit cold…" Mary began.

Ian reached past her and opened the door. "Shall we go in?" he asked with a smile.

"Only if you order for me, because I know I'm going to say it wrong," she said.

"Deal," he said with a chuckle.

They were led to a comfortable table in the corner, and Mary excused herself immediately to use the Ladies Room. Ian studied the menu for a moment before the waitress approached his table. "Do you know what your wife would like?" she asked.

"Let me see," he said. "A small pasty, a slice of cherry pie and a diet..." He stopped, shook his head and smiled at the waitress, who nearly swooned. "No, the diet's off the table because of the baby." He studied the menu again and, not finding what he was looking for, looked up at the woman again. "Do you have a bit of herbal tea?"

"Honey, if we didn't have it, I would run to the store and get you some myself," she said. "I think we've got chamomile. Would that work?"

"That would be fine," he replied. "And thank you."

The waitress walked away from the table and met Mary as she was coming back from the restroom. "You got yourself a keeper there," the waitress said.

Mary smiled and nodded. "Yes, I do," she said.

"I've got myself a keeper?" Mary asked quietly. Ian stood up and waited while Mary slipped into her chair.

"Ah, well, she assumed you were my wife, and it just seemed like a lot of work to explain," he replied, sitting after her. "And, you know, you have been my wife in the past."

She smiled. "Well, that was before I was married."

He chuckled. "Aye, that's true," he said. "I hope you don't mind. I ordered for you."

She shook her head. "So, what am I getting?"

"Well, Bradley also told me that you ought to be eating plenty of protein, some high fiber, dark green vegetables and stay away from too much sugar," he explained.

Mary sighed. "So, what am I eating?"

"A small pasty, a large piece of pie and a cup of tea," he said. "I nearly ordered the Diet Pepsi, but I knew you'd sworn off."

Grinning at him, Mary nodded. "You can be my husband any time you want to," she said. "Thank you."

"Oh, and the pasty comes with a wee bit of cole-slaw, so you've got your veggies in case Bradley asks."

"You are sneaky and brilliant," Mary said.

"Auch, well now, you're going to swell my head," he teased. Then he looked up and saw the waitress approaching with their tea. "I wonder if she knows anything about the fire?"

"You should ask her," Mary whispered. "She's got a crush on you."

Ian looked up as the waitress placed the cups and saucers on the table. "Thank you so much," he said.

She smiled back. "Is there anything else you need until your order is up?"

"Actually, well, I was wondering something," Ian said. "We're in town doing a little research for a project I'm working on. And I was wondering if you knew anyone we could speak to about the Lancaster fire."

She stared at him for a moment. "The Lancaster Family fire?" she asked.

"Aye," he said. "We don't want to open any wounds, but believe me, it's very important."

She turned away from them for a moment, and Mary was sure she was going to walk away. But instead, she pulled a chair from a nearby table and started to sit down next to their table. "I lived next door to the Lancasters," she said. "Ask away."

Chapter Twenty-one

Ian quickly stood up and waited until the waitress was seated before he sat down.

"Well, ain't you the polite one," the waitress commented. She turned to Mary. "It's that whole continental thing, isn't it?"

Mary nodded. "Yes. Yes, it is," she agreed. "So, you really lived next door to the Lancasters?"

"Yes, I was just a kid," she said. "But I still remember it like it was yesterday."

Ian started to say something, and then he stopped. "Before we continue this, I have to ask, is this fine with your employer?" he asked. "I would hate to have you reprimanded for helping us."

"Oh, honey, I own this place," she said. "I'm the Marge of Marge's Diner, and I can take a break whenever I want. 'Sides, it's slow as molasses in here right now. So, you go ahead and question me." Then she turned away from them and called to the other waitress on duty. "Annie, you watch for their order, hear? And when it's up, bring me a diet, too."

Ian saw Mary look at the woman with envy. Then she picked up her tea and sipped. With a smile, Ian called to the other waitress too. "Annie, darling, would you make it two? And if you have a bit of lime or lemon to put in mine, I'd appreciate it."

Mary looked up, confused. "But you don't like…"

He winked at her. "You can't have a glass full, but certainly a wee sip won't hurt."

She brightened. Then she shook her head. "I really shouldn't," she replied.

"Aye, but you will, won't you?" Ian teased.

"Well, if you force me," she countered hopefully.

"Aye, I'm forcing you to at least have a sip," he said.

"Then I guess I'll have to," she replied, her smile wide. "Thank you."

"Sometimes you need a wee bit of cheating for comfort," he said. Then he turned to the waitress. "Now, you couldn't have been more than a babe in arms when this happened."

Marge smiled. "Actually, I was nine," she said. "A little younger than Tony. But I still get chills."

"Why?" Mary asked.

"Tony wasn't like regular kids," she said. "And it wasn't like he had a mean streak, you know, like some boys do. He was just emotionless. He would torture little animals, like a neighbor's cat, just to do it. Just to watch the animal suffer. And he was always watching you." She shivered. "My mom used to bring us kids into the house when Tony was outside."

"How long did he live next door to you?" Ian asked.

"Well, now, come to think of it," she mused, "they didn't live there all that long. As a matter of fact, I think there was some stir up in the town where they used to live, so they moved here to Flynt in a big hurry. I remember my mom mentioning that."

"Perhaps something that Tony did?" Mary asked.

Marge nodded. "Yeah, something he did to another child in school," she said slowly. "Now that I remember that, it even seems scarier."

Anne approached the table with their order and the two glasses of Diet Pepsi. She placed the order on the table and put one of the glasses next to Ian. He took the straw out of the paper wrapping, put it in the glass and slid it over next to Mary. She leaned down, sipped the soda and closed her eyes in delight. "Oh, I really missed that taste," she said. Then she pushed it away.

"You've been off soda for how long?" Marge asked.

Mary glanced down at her belly. "About eight months," she said. "And I've been really good so far."

Marge cocked her head towards Ian. "So, this one's a bad influence?" she teased.

Mary shook her head. "No, he is an expert on people, what makes them tick and what gives them hope," she said. "And, he understands that when people are under a lot of stress, sometimes a little comfort in the form of a bad habit can remove some of the tension."

Marge smiled. "He's pretty smart then?" she asked.

"He's a genius," Mary replied.

"Well, now, enough about me," Ian interrupted. "Marge, how were the rest of the family? Did they seem to have the same odd habits as Tony?"

"No, they didn't," she said. "Matter of fact, they all seemed almost afraid of him. I remember the mother pleading with him, bribing him, to come in for dinner, and he just stood outside playing her. Even at eight, I couldn't understand why she didn't just haul him in and whip his butt."

"Because he'd find a way to get even," Mary said.

"Yes," Marge said. "I suppose you're right. And, eventually he did. Killed them all whilst they were sleeping. Cold-blooded murder, that's what the court said."

"What happened to Tony?" Ian asked.

"He got sent away to the County Asylum," she said. "The juvie hall was too low security, and he was too young for the adult prison. 'Sides, everyone knew he was nuts. So he got locked up in there."

"Then what happened?" Mary asked.

"I heard he died in there," Marge said. "He didn't last too long. I heard it was suicide, but folks covered it up."

"Suicide?" Mary asked, turning to Ian. "Why would someone like that commit suicide?"

"That's a very good question," he said. "And I think it's a very important answer to get."

Chapter Twenty-two

After lunch, Ian and Mary decided to cross the street and visit the small Flynt library. The library consisted of one long room with shelves that bisected areas of interest; fiction, non-fiction, children and mixed media. They immediately walked over to the circulation desk to speak with the librarian. The librarian, a middle-aged woman with a permanent frown, looked up from her computer and stared at them. "Yes?" she asked curtly.

Ian put on his most charming smile. "Hello, we're doing some research, and we were wondering if you might help us," he said.

"Did you check the computers first?" she asked. "Most of what you need can be found on the computers if you only take the time to look."

"Actually, it would be research in your local history section," he said calmly. "Unless those files have been added to your computer database."

"No, they haven't," she said. Then she looked back at her computer screen.

Ian and Mary waited for a few moments for her to continue the conversation, but she was already typing away. Mary felt her temper rise. "Excuse me," she said. "Are you or are you not the librarian who is paid to work here?"

The woman looked up, surprised. "I am," she said.

"Well, good. I'm glad we have that established," Mary replied. "Now, we asked you a question about the local history collection. Would you please reply?"

"I already did," she snapped. "I told you the collection was not put on the database."

"So how can we see the collection?" Mary asked.

"Well, if you had bothered to look at the information on the front door, you would have seen that the local history room is only open one day a week, and that day was yesterday," she said. "So, come back next week and try again."

"Isn't there someone you can call to help us with the information?" Ian asked.

"You don't live around here, do you?" she asked.

Ian and Mary shook their heads. "No," Ian said. "Why?"

"Well, if you don't live around here, you don't pay taxes. So, you don't pay my salary or the salary of the local history librarian," she said tightly.

"So, we will not call someone in to help you. You can come back next week. Good day."

"Why you…" Mary began, but before she could continue, Ian had pulled her away from the circulation desk and guided her to the front door.

"I cannot believe her attitude," Mary said. "She ought to be fired."

Ian nodded. "Aye, but it's a small town," he said. "And if someone is as rude as she and still has a job, it must be that she's related to someone else higher up who's protecting her."

Mary nodded slowly. "Her brother is the mayor," she said.

He smiled. "Or something like that," he agreed.

"I bet the people in this town all subscribe to Amazon to get their books," Mary grumbled.

Ian laughed. "Aye, I'd rather pay good money than face the she-dragon in her lair," he said.

They stood on Main Street and then walked back to his car. "So, what shall we do next?" Ian asked.

"We could find the house and settle in before it gets dark," Mary suggested. "Then, perhaps, we could take a trip out to the asylum."

Ian nodded. "I'm fine with that," he said, opening her car door for her. "Something tells me that the asylum is going to be a little less frightening now that Tony is in Freeport."

Mary shivered and ran her hands up and down her arms before she climbed in the car. "Don't remind me," she said. "When I think that he could be targeting our house…"

"Don't worry," Ian said. "Between Bradley, Mike and the equipment Wyatt left for them, they'll be fine."

Ian closed her door, walked over to his side and climbed in. Then he turned to her. "Really, they will be fine."

She sighed and nodded. "But the sooner we figure out his whole story, the sooner we'll be able to decide how to deal with him."

Chapter Twenty-three

Ian followed the directions Bradley had given him and soon turned onto a quiet, tree-lined residential street a few blocks from Main Street. The house was in the center of a cul-de-sac at the end of the block. Ian pulled the car around the cul-de-sac and into the gravel driveway next to the tiny cottage.

"This is like a fairytale cottage," Mary exclaimed. The house was one-story but had a tall, steepled roof with a cobblestone fireplace extending along one side. The front door was curved on top, and the edging around the doorway was cobblestone. There were beds for flowers, now covered with snow, on either side of the tiny front porch, and shrubs and miniature trees all along the curved walkway to the house.

Ian helped her out of the car and then picked up both of their suitcases. "Best be wary, Mary," he said softly. "Remember the wicked witch that caged Hansel and Gretel? She lived in a fairy tale cottage, too."

Mary turned to him and shook her head. "I could so take her," she said with a grin and started up the path to the house.

Ian put the suitcases down on the porch and handed Mary the key. She inserted it into the lock, opened the door and gasped in delight. The inside looked like a fairytale with a large fireplace against one wall inside a cozy little parlor that had pictures of dark forests and shining castles. The walls were stenciled with fairy tales, and the windows were all mullioned. The floors were polished wood with faded, pastel, Oriental rugs, and the kitchen had a sturdy, wooden table of polished oak that sat in a nook overlooking the backyard. The kitchen stove was a replica of an old-fashioned wood burner, with a red, shiny enamel coating, and the cabinets were oak with glass panes.

"This is just magical," Mary said. "I wonder which of Bradley's friends owns it."

Ian put the suitcases down in the hallway and looked around. "This is definitely not what I think of when I think of a hunting cabin."

"Unless, of course, you're hunting fairies," Mary teased.

The stark look in Ian's face shocked her. "Ian, are you okay?" she asked immediately.

He shook his head quickly, and the look disappeared. "Sorry. Yes. I'm fine," he said.

He looked around again. "So do you think your bedroom has a bed with twenty mattresses and twenty eiderdown feather beds?" he asked, referring to the Princess and the Pea story.

Mary chuckled and laid her hands on her belly. "I hope not. Unless you consider Mikey a pea in a pod," she replied.

"Well, let's find out," he said, picking up her suitcase and going down the hallway to the first bedroom.

The bedroom was as magical as the rest of the house, with a four poster, brass bed in the middle of the room with a high-topped, feather mattress and a quilt depicting the Swan Princess. The room was decorated in ivory and golds from the curtains to the vanity and dresser. The rug next to the bed was thick, shearling wool, and the lamp on the nightstand was in the shape of a swan.

"Wow," Mary said. "Just wow." She turned to Ian, who had laid her suitcase on a bench behind her bed. "I'm almost afraid to climb onto the bed for fear I'll never want to get off."

"Doesn't this seem a little odd to you?" he asked. "This is not a man's cabin."

She nodded. "It does seem a little too good to be true," she agreed. "But maybe that's just a coincidence. Maybe this is my reward for not slapping the librarian."

Ian chuckled and shook his head. "No, because your intent was to slap her," he said. "I was the one who saved the day."

"Okay. I can admit that," Mary agreed. "Maybe this is your reward and I just get to be here too." She grabbed his hand and pulled him out of her room. "Come on, let's see what your room looks like."

She was halfway down the hall when she stopped, and Ian nearly ran into her back.

"Oh my," Mary whispered.

The ghost, a graceful, older woman with soft white curls, sparkling blue eyes and a gentle smile, looked just as surprised as Mary. "Oh my, indeed."

Chapter Twenty-four

"Is this your home?" Mary asked the ghost. "It's just beautiful."

The ghost studied Mary calmly and then nodded. "Yes, it is," she said. "And thank you. I spent years getting it just the way I wanted. May I ask why you're here?"

"A friend of my husband lent us the house for the week," Mary explained.

The ghost looked at Mary and then beyond her to Ian. "Isn't it a little unusual for a husband to allow his wife to stay in a house with another man?"

Ian coughed lightly and stepped forward. "Aye, it is," he agreed. "But Mary and I have a unique skill, and as it turns out, we're working together."

She smiled at Ian. "Edinburgh, correct?" she asked. "With a little time in the outer Hebrides?"

He nodded. "You've got a keen ear," he replied. "Aye, I grew up near Edinburgh, but we summered in the Hebrides."

"I love accents of the world," she explained. "I loved studying them." She grinned, her nose crinkling in the process. "I just loved studying everything. Now, what are you working on? Perhaps I could help."

Mary couldn't imagine how this petite, older woman, now a ghost, could aid in their investigation, and she wondered if the woman even realized that she was dead. "Before we go any further," Mary said, "can you remember the last thing you did?"

The woman turned to Mary and smiled. "Oh, my dear, are you trying to determine if I know I'm dead?" she asked, a twinkle in her eyes. "Why how very thoughtful. But, yes, I am quite aware of my other-worldly status. Although, I must admit that I'm quite surprised to have an intelligent conversation with the two of you."

Ian grinned. "Because we're mortals?" he asked.

She chuckled. "Well, in my past life I have to admit that intelligent conversations were few and far between," she agreed. "But, no, I'm surprised that you can see me and that you aren't falling over yourselves to get away. The new fellow who lays claim to my house tends to be frightened quite easily."

"He does?" Mary asked.

"Well, really, I spent years creating this lovely fairytale cottage, and he comes in with paint to cover up the stencils on the walls," she said. "What would you expect me to do but move those paint cans back outside the house."

"In front of him?" Mary asked, trying to hide a smile.

The woman giggled, a soft, joyous sound. "I do admit that had I been him, floating paint cans might have frightened me, too," she said, and then she added with a smile. "He hasn't been around too much lately."

Ian coughed again, hiding his laughter. "I'm sure it was a bit of a surprise," he agreed.

She laughed and nodded. "That would be an understatement," she said.

"Why are you still here?" Mary asked. "Are you just protecting your home?"

The woman smiled. "Now wouldn't this home be a lovely heaven for me?" she asked. "Did you see my bookshelves? Filled with all of my favorite books. I really could spend eternity here. But, no, I actually have been to the light, and it was superb. However, I find myself on some kind of assignment. I need to be here, for some reason."

"Perhaps we're the reason for your presence," Ian said. "We're trying to learn more about Tony Lancaster."

"Oh, that troubled young man that killed his family?" she asked. "Yes, I know a great deal about him." She paused for a moment. "Oh, how rude of me. I never did introduce myself. My name is Adeline McKinley. I was a professor at the University of Wisconsin, and when I retired, I moved here and was the librarian until my death."

"Oh, you would have been so much better than..." Mary stopped and clapped her hand over her mouth.

Adeline laughed and shrugged. "Yes, I know," she said. "I've visited and seen the new librarian in action."

"Is she related to someone in power?" Ian asked.

Chuckling, Adeline nodded. "Yes, the mayor's sister," she said. "How did you know?"

"No one that lacking in basic, genteel deportment could hold a position like that unless they had connections," Ian said.

She smiled in approval at him. "Very well said," she replied. "And you are..."

"And now we have been impolite," Ian remarked. "I am Ian McDougal, and I too am a professor, from the University of Edinburgh. And this lovely lady is my good friend and colleague Mary O'Reilly Alden."

"It's lovely to meet you, and I'm elated to have you staying in my home," she replied. "Now, shall we plan on going back to the library this evening, after hours?"

"But how can we—" Mary started.

"Oh, I kept a key," Adeline inserted. "And I've been haunting the place for months." She looked at both of them and shook her head. "I was not happy with my replacement. So, due to my overt displays of paranormal ability, no one comes near the library at night." She grinned widely. "I believe I terrify them."

"I wonder if that would work for overdue books," Mary mused.

Adeline laughed loudly. "Oh, I hadn't given that a thought," she said. "Perhaps that's my next assignment."

"When does the library close?" Ian asked.

"At nine o'clock tonight," she replied. "And, nowadays, they leave promptly at closing. But, to be safe, we shouldn't visit until about ten."

"And there is information about Tony Lancaster?" Mary asked.

"I created a file, just about the Lancaster case," Adeline said. "I was very intrigued by the entire situation, so I kept clippings from the trials as well as later articles that tried to understand his behavior."

"That would be very useful," Ian said. "We were going to visit the asylum this evening, but after that, a visit to the library would be ideal."

"Wonderful," Adeline said. "It will be so fun to visit the library with company. I didn't realize how much I missed conversation."

She smiled sadly and shook her head. "You just don't get a lot of chance for conversation when you're dead."

Chapter Twenty-five

"Mike, will you just stop talking for a minute while I figure this thing out?" Bradley asked as he sat on the floor in Clarissa's room putting together a monitor to record both audio and video.

"It shouldn't be all that difficult," Mike said, hovering over Bradley's shoulder. "I mean, the thing is made for a baby."

Bradley looked up and glared at Mike. "It's made to use in a baby's room," he said. "That doesn't mean a baby can operate it."

"And neither can a full-grown man, obviously," Mike replied. "Maybe you should call Katie Brennan over. She's really good at these kinds of things."

Gritting his teeth, Bradley took a deep breath. "I will get it put together myself," he said. "I only need a few moments of quiet to concentrate."

"Oh. Sorry. You mean you want me to be quiet, right?" Mike asked, a twinkle of mischief in his eyes.

Bradley nodded. "Yes. You. Quiet," Bradley replied as he held up one of the six connectors and tried to find the corresponding attachment.

Mike glided away from Bradley, sat on the bed and started to whistle.

Bradley looked over his shoulder and stared, incredulously, at Mike.

"What?" Mike asked, and then he nodded. "Oh. Sorry. Quiet. That's right."

Bradley turned back and held up the connector. "It would be a lot more helpful if the instructions were in English," he muttered, turning one of the pieces upside down.

"Bradley," Mike said.

"No. Not a word," Bradley replied as he lifted the other piece and studied it.

"Um, Bradley," Mike tried again.

"Mike, could you just maybe go downstairs and watch for Clarissa?" Bradley said.

"Wow. Okay. If you don't mind hurting my feelings," Mike replied.

Bradley put the pieces on the floor and looked at Mike. "I don't mind hurting your feelings," he said.

Mike stood. "Fine, then I won't tell you that the English instructions are under your left knee," he said, and then he disappeared from the room.

Bradley moved his knee and saw the instructions, in English, laying on the floor. He closed his eyes and sighed deeply. "Mike," he called loudly. "Mike, I'm sorry."

There was no answer.

"Mike," he called again. "I was a jerk. I'm sorry."

He waited. Again there was no answer.

Looking down at the pile of electronics at his feet, he shook his head, stood up and walked out the door into the hallway. "Mike," he called, going down the stairs. "I said I was…"

He stopped halfway down the steps and stared in dismay. The top tier of the Christmas tree was now empty, and all of the ornaments Mary had so carefully chosen to be placed up high were scattered in pieces on the ground. "What happened?" he gasped.

Mike shook his head. "I can only guess that our shadow visitor is not fond of Christmas trees," he said.

Bradley came down the rest of the steps into the room. "It wasn't Lucky?" he asked.

"No, I checked on her immediately. Lucky's in the corner of the kitchen, pretty freaked out," Mike replied. "It wasn't her."

Bradley looked down and sighed with regret. The antique, blown-glass ornament that had been passed down from his great-grandmother was shattered and in pieces. He bent down and picked up the largest piece.

"I'm so sorry," Mike said.

Bradley studied the piece, stood up and then placed it reverently on the mantle. He turned to Mike, his face set. "He caught us off guard," he said. "And we can't let that happen again. Were you just giving me a hard time when you mentioned Katie Brennan was good at electronics?"

Mike nodded. "I was giving you a hard time," he said. "But she's amazing at electronics. She has a knack."

"How much time before the kids are out of school?" Bradley asked.

Mike glanced over to the clock. "You've got a good couple of hours," he said.

Bradley pulled his phone out of his pocket and pressed a number. "Hi, Katie," he said. "It's Bradley. I was wondering if you could help me with something here at the house."

Chapter Twenty-six

The asylum was only a few miles out of town in the countryside, and it was still light when they arrived. Ian parked the Range Rover on the dirt access road near the asylum, and they both sat in the vehicle and stared at the building, remembering their last encounter.

"Well, it looks slightly less creepy in the daytime," Mary said.

Ian nodded slowly. "Only slightly, though," he said. He turned to her. "You know, you don't have to go inside if you don't want to. I can go in and see if I can find any records or anything else."

"Ian," she said with a shake of her head. "Do you remember what Mike said the last time we were here? They can already feel my presence, so if you leave me out here, I'm bound to have company."

"Are you sure?" he asked.

"I'm sure," she replied. "Besides, with two of us, the investigation will be quicker and more thorough."

They walked together up the snow-covered path to the old building. "The last time you were here, you felt lightheaded," Ian said. "How are you feeling now?"

Mary took a deep breath and shrugged. "Good," she said. "I feel good. I mean, I can feel some spiritual presence, but I don't feel like it's weighing down on me this time."

"That's probably a good sign that Tony hasn't followed us back here to Wisconsin," Ian said. He helped Mary up the crumbling steps of the asylum and then brushed the snow off the combination lock with his gloved hand. He entered the numbers Dee had sent them, and the lock opened easily.

They both pulled the heavy chain out from within the door handles, and then Ian stepped up and placed his hands on the handles. "Before we go in, let's turn on our flashlights," he said.

Mary nodded and flipped on her high-powered LED flashlight. "Yes, I remember those doors slamming shut behind us," she said. "And I would not like to be standing in the dark in that building."

Once their flashlights were on, Ian pressed down on the handles and pushed open the doors. This time, the doors opened smoothly, but under Ian's power, not by a supernatural force. They carefully stepped inside and moved forward. The large doors remained open, spilling daylight into the lobby.

"Better and better," Ian remarked. "But we shouldn't let our guard down."

Mary nodded. "Right there with you," she agreed.

They moved to the center of the old lobby with its art deco style, black and white tile floor, careful to step over the cracked tiles, and shined their flashlights around the room. "So far just a scary, old building," Mary commented. "Which way do you want to go?"

Ian slowly ran his flashlight around the lobby. There were two hallways that led from the lobby into the rest of the asylum. The one Mary had taken last time was on the left of the room, and the one the rest of the group had taken was to the right.

"What was down your hall?" Ian asked.

"There were some operating rooms," Mary said, shivering quickly as she remembered the procedures she'd witnessed. "And a lot of closed doors."

"Could they have been offices?" Ian asked.

"Yes, they could have been," Mary agreed. "Offices with file cabinets, right?"

He smiled at her. "Right," he said. "Are you okay with going back down that hall?"

She sighed. "Ian, I'm pregnant, not made of glass," she said. "And although I'm really touched by your concern, I really wish you'd…"

"Bugger off?" he replied with a smile.

She laughed and nodded. "But in a polite way," she added.

"You're right," he agreed. "Sorry. I just have been a little obsessive about protecting the people in my life."

She slipped her arm through his and leaned against him for a moment. "And I know that it's only because you care," she said.

"Aye, but I need to remember that you are capable and strong," he said. He took a deep breath and nodded. "Okay, let's do this."

"Okay!" she replied.

They took the hall to the left. It was lined with yellowing wall tiles and more black and white floor tiles. The plaster above the tiles was peeling, and there was dirt and debris scattered on the floor.

"Lovely place," Mary whispered. "No windows, no natural light. It would have been like living in a cave."

Ian nodded. "I wonder if this environment didn't make the residents even worse," he replied.

"I wondered that myself."

Mary looked at Ian in surprise, and they both turned around to find a tall, thin ghost standing in front of one of the closed doors they had just passed. He was wearing a lab coat over his shirt and tie, and dress slacks and black, leather shoes completed his attire. His brown hair was just graying at the edges, and he wore it in a military, crew-cut style. His eyeglasses were round and wire-rimmed and perched on the end on his nose.

"Hello," Ian said. "I don't believe I've met you. I'm Professor Ian McDougal, and I'm doing research on the Lancaster case."

The ghost sighed deeply. "I'm afraid I failed with that case," he said, his voice thick with regret. "The boy killed himself, and I didn't even see it coming."

"Hello, I'm Mary O'Reilly Alden," Mary said. "Can we chat with you about your findings? Because he's dead, there are no HIPAA regulations that we need to worry about."

"I'm sorry, what?" the ghost asked.

Ian turned to Mary and whispered, "HIPAA didn't happen until 1996. If I guess correctly, we are meeting Dr. Buus, and he died in the eighties."

Then Ian turned to the ghost. "Are you Dr. Buus?" he asked.

The ghost smiled and nodded. "Mark. Please call me Mark," he replied. He looked slowly around and shook his head. "This place has really gone downhill fast."

"Do you know what year it is?" Mary asked.

He smiled at her. "You would have made an excellent psychiatrist," he said. "Asking leading questions to get information not having anything to do with the answer. But, to answer your unspoken question, yes, I realize I'm dead. Although, I can admit, I don't remember a lot about the circumstances surrounding my death at this point."

"And have you seen a light?" Ian asked.

His smile widened. "Ah, the proverbial passageway to heaven," he said. "No, I haven't, and believe me, I've looked. So, either there is no such thing or I still have unfinished business here on earth."

"There's a light," Mary said with confidence. "So, let's go with the unfinished business. Can we talk to you about Tony?"

He nodded. "Yes, come into my office," he invited. "There's a lot I can share."

Chapter Twenty-seven

Mark slipped through the door. Then Ian opened it for he and Mary to go through. The office, like the rest of the building, showed obvious signs of deterioration. Plaster was peeling in large pieces from the wall; the linoleum was yellowed and pulling away from the floor. The turquoise Naugahyde chairs still placed in front of the old, metal desk were brittle and torn, but still capable of use. Ian picked up one, turned it upside down to get rid of the debris on it and then set it down for Mary.

"My lady," he teased with a bow.

She smiled. "Why, thank you," she replied, perching on the edge of the chair.

He did the same for his own chair, and they sat across from Mark, who was seated on an invisible chair on the other side of the table. Clasping his hands together, Mark leaned towards them. "First, I need to apologize that everything I'm going to share with you is from my memory," he said, glancing over to an old, five-drawer, black, steel, filing cabinet in the corner of the room. "I've tried everything to open it, but I can't. And beyond that, I'm afraid I've lost the key."

Ian glanced at Mary, and she nodded. "Go ahead," she encouraged him.

He stood, pulled a small sheath from his back pocket and opened it to reveal a number of small, metal tools. He turned to Mark. "May I have a go at it?" he asked.

"Yes, please, do try," Mark agreed.

Ian pulled out a thin, pointed tool and slipped it into the keyhole. Then he pulled out a flatter tool and slipped it on top, jiggling the tool as it penetrated the small, grey housing. In a moment, they were rewarded by the sound of a click, and the locking device popped forward, unlocking the cabinet.

"Which drawer?" Ian asked.

Mark smiled and sighed with satisfaction. "The second drawer," he said. "The large file towards the back."

Ian opened the drawer and was grateful to see that all the files were intact. "Fireproof," he commented, examining the drawer. "That's what saved them. This cabinet is fireproof."

"What do you mean?" Mark asked.

"You died in a fire," Mary said. "But, from your appearance, I would guess that you died of smoke inhalation, rather than burns."

"Why would you assume that?" he asked.

"I've had a lot of experience with…" she paused, searching for the right word.

"Ghosts?" Mark supplied.

She smiled and nodded. "Yes, actually, ghosts," she replied. "And I've learned that their images as spirits, spirits still earth-bound, retain the same appearance they had when they died."

"So, a hanging victim..." Mark ventured.

Mary squinted in distaste and nodded. "Yeah, it isn't a pretty sight," she said. "So, the fact that you are unscarred and your clothes are fine tells me it was smoke inhalation, rather than incineration."

"Well, there's something to be grateful for," he quipped. "But, it's very interesting to learn that I was a victim of fire. Did you know that many others in this institution were also victims of fire?"

Ian placed the large file on the desk and sat down. "Yes, actually, the guard at the courthouse mentioned that," Ian said.

"And did he also mention that all of those victims had a relationship in one way or another with Tony Lancaster?" Mark asked.

"Um, no," Mary said. "He didn't mention that at all."

Mark templed his hands together and was lost in thought for a moment. Finally, he looked up and met Ian's eyes. "I read something once about psychotic individuals and a connection to psychic abilities. Have you ever heard anything about that?"

Ian nodded. "Aye, I have," he said. "There were a number of cases involving individuals who were serial killers and later diagnosed as psychotic, that showed evidence of precognition, telekinesis and even clairvoyance."

"Tony Lancaster was not only psychotic, but also brilliant," Mark said. "He tested off the charts in intelligence."

"Common for psychotic individuals," Ian added.

"That's right. That's right," Mark said. "And the way I learned about the link between psychotic behavior and psychic ability is because I found articles in Tony's room, scholarly articles describing the testing and the behaviors."

He flipped open the file and pulled out several paperclipped articles. "I put them in his file after I finished reading them myself," he said. "And then I discovered that he had obtained a game, Kreskin's ESP. Have you ever heard of it?"

Ian nodded. "Yes, actually, I have one back home in Edinburgh," he said. "It has a series of games, for lack of a better word, that test your psychic ability."

Mark nodded. "Exactly. Tests and then, perhaps, improves them," he said. "Tony was actually way above average when reading the cards. He could shuffle them, lay them face down on a surface and then point to them with very little thought and correctly identify the hidden shapes."

"How above average?" Ian asked.

"Generally, 100 percent accurate," Mark replied. "Unless he was distracted and lost concentration. Then the percentage decreased."

"So, if Tony knew or felt that he had this kind of power, why would he decide to commit suicide?" Mary asked.

Mark looked back down at the file and shuffled through the papers, finally finding one and sliding it onto the desk in front of them. "I believe it was because of this," he said.

Mary and Ian looked at the paper. Mary gasped softly. The headline of the article read, "Psychic Power Increases After Death."

Chapter Twenty-eight

With the file safely tucked inside Ian's coat, he and Mary slid the chains back through the door handles and secured the combination lock to them. Then Ian turned to Mary. "How's your connection to Mike these days?" he asked. Then he helped her down the slick stairs.

"Pretty good, I think," she replied, stepping down and then walking alongside him towards the car. "Why?"

"I'd like to chat with him for a few moments," he replied, shining his flashlight down the darkened path. "And the sooner, the better."

"Can we get in the warm car first?" Mary suggested hopefully.

He smiled and nodded. "Of course," he said.

He helped her inside the vehicle, then quickly went around to the other side to get in and turn it on. Almost immediately, warm air started to circulate inside the interior. Mary, holding her hands up to the vent, turned and smiled at him. "Perfect," she said.

She took a deep breath, cleared her mind and then pictured Mike.

"You called?" Mike asked as he appeared in the back seat.

"That was fast," Mary said.

"Well, I have to admit that I was anxiously awaiting a call all day," Mike replied. "So, what's up."

"We think we've found our ghost," Ian said. "But we've encountered a couple of concerns."

"I'm sure he's the boy from my dreams," Mary said. "So he does have a connection to me."

"And not only was he diagnosed as with psychotic tendencies but he also may have had highly attuned psychic abilities," Ian added. "Which may have continued beyond life."

"So, if he's tuning into Mary," Mike said, "he might be able to tell that she's not in Freeport."

Ian nodded. "I'm assuming that you put enough fear in him that he hasn't come by yet," Ian said. "But if he starts searching…"

"Yeah, yeah, I get you," Mike replied. "So, what we need is a psychic decoy."

"You can do that?" Mary asked.

He turned to her and smiled. "Sure, you're just a mixture of compassion, goodness, courage, empathy, humor and kindness," he said. "Piece of cake. Hmmmm, for added sweetness, I could use a cake."

"So, you're like a fairy godmother, turning something inanimate into something real?" she teased, touched and flattered by his words.

"But, you know, considering your current state, I could also use a pumpkin," he teased.

"Oh, well, all those nice things I was thinking about you," she said in mock anger. "They are completely gone."

He chuckled. "How's the rest going?" he asked.

"We've had a number of very interesting encounters," Ian replied. "But everything has been very positive."

Mike sobered when he turned to Ian. "Not all of those encounters are happenstance," he said meaningfully. "Sometimes God works in mysterious ways."

"Aye, I've been on the end of some of those mysterious ways," Ian said, a little bit of bitterness in his tone. "But I'll take whatever help I can get."

"How's everyone at home?" Mary asked.

"Missing you," Mike said. Then he turned to Ian. "Actually, both of you. Clarissa was very disappointed to come home and discover you'd gone."

Ian softened. "She's a gem," he said. "Tell her I miss her, too."

Mike nodded. "I will," he said. Then he turned to Mary. "And if you ever need me, just whistle. You know how to whistle, don't you, Mary? You just put your lips together and blow."

She grinned at him. "You do a more believable Bogart than Bacall," she teased.

He nodded. "Yeah, I really wish Bogie had said that line," he laughed as he started to fade away. "Be safe. Both of you."

Mary waited until Ian had backed out of the dirt driveway and was back on the paved road. "So, Ian," she said.

"Yes, Mary, darling," he replied on cue.

"Just how do we stop a psychotic ghost with psychic abilities who has been able to murder people even after death?"

"That, my dear, is the question of the night," he replied, his voice losing any shred of levity. "The question of the night."

Chapter Twenty-nine

"This is a lovely vehicle," Adeline said as she sat in the back seat of the Range Rover on their way to the library. "Is this real leather?"

Ian chuckled. "Aye, it is," he said. "And if you were a little more substantial, I would have turned on the seat warmers back there."

"Really, seat warmers in the back," she sighed. "Well, that is luxurious."

"Once we got seat warmers in our car," Mary said, "I wondered how I ever lived without them."

Adeline chuckled. "It is human nature for luxuries to become necessities after a little while," she said.

She glanced out the window. "Oh, why don't you park over there, in the Piggly Wiggly parking lot," she suggested. "Then no one will notice a car near the library."

Ian pulled into the supermarket's lot and parked close to the street. He turned in his seat. "Should we wait a wee bit?" he asked.

Adeline shook her head. "Oh, no, it's after ten," she said. "During this time of year, the only thing open after ten is the Piggly Wiggly. So, if we just walk along this side street and then cut through the alleyway, you should be just fine."

Following her direction, they were at the back of the library in a few minutes. Ian pulled the key Adeline had given him from his pocket, and Mary carefully shielded her flashlight beam so it illuminated the lock, but nothing else. The lock clicked and the doorknob turned. Ian glanced over his shoulder and smiled victoriously at Mary, then proceeded to push the door open. But the movement was stopped by a chain-lock on the other side. Ian tried again, but the chain held.

"Oh my," Adeline said, shaking her head. "Why would they put a chain on the door?"

"Perhaps to prevent people from breaking in," Mary suggested, trying not to laugh.

Adeline glanced over at her. "Some people laugh at the most inappropriate moments," she commented, trying to keep her lips from twitching too. "And I suppose I'm one of them."

Mary laughed softly, but then stopped when she could see that Ian was not as amused as they were. "Oh, sorry," she said.

"I dinna think I want to be found at the back door of the library with a fairly hysterical pregnant woman as my accomplice," he said.

Mary turned to Adeline. "His Scottish gets more pronounced when he's stressed," she explained. "I noticed that about him."

"Mary," Ian said, not sounding amused.

"Do you think I should just pop into the library and unhook the chain?" Adeline asked with a giggle. "Before the Professor loses it?"

"I think that would be a wonderful idea," Mary replied.

Ian pulled the door closed and sighed, loudly. They heard the clank of the chain hitting the surface of the door just as the policeman made himself known.

"Excuse me," he said. "May I help you?"

"Oops," Mary whispered.

"Good evening, officer," Ian said. "Fine night for a walk, isn't it?"

The officer took a stance next to them, his arms on his hips and his face unsmiling. "No, actually. It's damn cold out here," he said.

Mary moved out from behind Ian and smiled. "I'm afraid this is all my fault," she explained. She placed her mittened hands over her protruding belly and smiled up at the officer. "I had a craving for dark chocolate ice cream, so we drove to the Piggly Wiggly to pick some out." She leaned closer to the officer and lowered her voice. "He never seems to be able to pick out the right kind, so I insist on coming."

"But the Piggly Wiggly is over there," the officer said, motioning with his head.

"Yes, that's true," she said. "And actually, we haven't even been inside the store yet to buy the ice cream because today, when we were shopping, one of the clerks told me that the library was haunted. I'm really interested in paranormal things. I watch all of those shows on television, you know like Ghost Discoverers. I even got to meet Dee, the new star of that show." She took a deep breath and continued. "So, I begged Ian to bring me over here so I could peek in the windows. I'm so sorry. I didn't even think that it would be against the law."

The officer studied Mary for a long moment and then turned to Ian. "Your first baby?" he asked.

Ian nodded. "Aye, it's been a long eight months."

The officer's lips twitched. "I remember my wife always needed Chinese food," he said. "In the middle of the night. I had to drive clear up to Madison to find an all-night Chinese place."

"What a wonderful husband you are," Mary said, and then she paused and turned to Ian. "Oh, you know, sweet and sour chicken sounds really good."

The officer laughed and sent a look of sympathy in Ian's direction. "They've got a deli in Piggly Wiggly that has pretty good Chinese," he said. "That will save you the trip to Madison."

"Thank you," Ian replied. "I really appreciate it."

Still chuckling, the officer tipped his hat at them. "Have a good night, folks," he said. "And if you go around to the side of the library, there's a window at shoulder height that will give you a better view."

"Thank you so much," Mary gushed.

"You're welcome, ma'am," he replied and continued down the alley.

"You are incorrigible," Ian whispered, his smile wide. "And my sympathy for Bradley has just increased tenfold. How he ever denies you anything is beyond me."

She smiled back. "Why, thank you," she replied without an ounce of guilt. "But, you know, Chinese really does sound good."

Chapter Thirty

The library door opened soundlessly behind him. "Hurry, get in before he comes back," Adeline called urgently.

With a furtive glance down the alley, just to be sure they were unnoticed, Ian nodded to Mary. "Okay, no one's watching," he said and let her slip into the darkened building before he hurried in, closing and locking the door behind him.

"Do you think the policeman will be back?" Mary asked Adeline.

Adeline nodded. "Most assuredly," she replied. "He takes his job very seriously. But the local history room has no windows, so we should be hidden in there."

"Has he seen you?" Ian asked.

Adeline smiled widely. "Yes, he has," she replied. "And he took it quite well. Just stared for a few long moments and then backed away from the window." She grinned at Mary. "The very window he suggested to look through."

She floated through the main stacks of the library, glowing softly so they didn't have to use a flashlight to see where they were going. "It was a pleasant surprise," Adeline continued. "Most law enforcement officials don't believe in ghosts."

Mary chuckled, instantly remembering Bradley's first reaction when she told him about ghosts. "But they can be taught," Mary whispered with a smile.

Ian glanced over and nodded. "Aye, and once they believe, they can become steadfast supporters," he said.

Adeline opened a door in the far back corner of the library and glided inside. Mary and Ian followed, and Ian closed the door behind them. As soon as the door was closed, a dim light came on, casting most of the room into shadows. The room was small, about ten feet by ten feet, with a number of old, file cabinets against one wall and two computer stations in the center of the room. On another wall, a large bookcase held local history books, as well as books written by local authors.

Mary looked around the room. "Where do we start?" she asked.

One of the file cabinet drawers opened. "Here," Adeline said, pointing at the drawer. "This is where I kept my file about Tony Lancaster."

Ian came up beside her, looked through the drawer and then pulled out a thick file. "This is impressive," he said.

"No," she replied. "That's just a start. I have three more files that size."

Ian placed the first file on an old, library table next to the file cabinets and then retrieved the other three. He put his hands on his hips and stared down at the collection. "I'd thought to take photos of the files," he said, shaking his head. "But going through all of this and taking photos would take all night."

"Well, why don't we just take them home?" Adeline asked.

"Don't you think they'll be missed?" Mary asked.

Adeline shook her head. "No, actually, the new librarian doesn't have a lot of use for the local history room," she explained. "The part-time librarian who is assigned to care for the collection generally has her hands full with restocking books and sending out fine notices when she does come in, work that, in my day, the head librarian did."

"And how do we return them, once we've borrowed them?" Ian asked.

Adeline smiled at them. "Why, you just explain that you found them in my house," she said, "while you were staying there. Heaven knows I took work home all the time. I just died before I could bring them back."

"That's brilliant," Mary replied. Then she glanced around. "But how do we get them out of here without making anyone suspicious?"

Adeline floated over to a small closet in the back of the room and opened the door. "This was my supply closet," she explained as she rustled through the items on the shelves. "And unless they've cleaned things out..." She paused for a moment.

"Here they are," she cried triumphantly, pulling out two brown shopping bags with the logo of Piggly Wiggly on the side. "These will be perfect cover for you."

Ian studied Adeline for a long moment. "Are you sure you weren't a spy before you became a librarian?"

Adeline met his eyes but didn't smile. "You will discover my past when it's time," she said to him.

"What do you mean?" he asked, confused.

"All in good time," she said with a finality that told Ian he was not going to get any more information from her that night. She nodded, and then her smile returned. "Now, then, let's pack these files up before we're discovered."

No sooner had she said those words than they heard a noise outside the room and light spilled in from underneath the doorway.

Chapter Thirty-one

"Crap," Mary whispered, reaching over and carefully turning the light off so it didn't make a sound.

"I'll see what's going on," Adeline said, gliding across the room and through the door.

"Bradley will not be pleased if I end up being arrested," Mary whispered.

"But not surprised, right?" Ian replied softly, with a twinkle in his eye.

Mary had to clap her hand over her mouth to hold back the laughter, but she shook her head at Ian. Finally, when she knew she could control the laughter, she removed her hand. "That was very rude of you," she whispered, a smile on her face. "But you're right. He wouldn't be surprised at all."

Adeline reappeared, her face filled with anger. "She's stealing," she shouted. "She's stealing from the library."

"Who?" Ian asked quietly.

"The mayor's sister, that's who," Adeline replied. "She's got a better salary than I ever had, she does nothing but play on the computer all day, and now she has the nerve to steal the funds from the library!"

Mary pulled out her phone and started to dial.

"What are you doing?" Ian asked.

"Calling the police," Mary replied.

"Are you forgetting that we are also illegally in the library and could get arrested?" he asked.

She paused for a moment, torn between pressing the call icon and saving themselves. She shook her head. "But, it's a library," Mary implored. "We can't let her steal the money."

Ian turned to Adeline. "You wouldn't happen to know the phone number of the police officer who stopped us?" he asked.

She nodded. "Yes, he gave it to me so I could call him when I had to work late," she said. "It's his private cell." She floated across the room, opened another drawer in the filing cabinet and pulled out an index card. "Here it is."

"Call him," Ian suggested.

Mary called the number and waited until it was picked up. "Hi, I'm the pregnant woman who was in the alley behind the library," she said. "I think that someone is breaking into the library." She paused. "How did I get your number?"

She looked beseechingly at Ian, who only shrugged. Then she took a deep breath. "Adeline gave it to me," she replied. "She is also the one who told me that the mayor's sister is stealing funds."

She paused, and a smile grew across her face. "Thank you," she said.

Hanging up the phone, she turned to them. "He's just around the corner, and he's coming through the front," she explained. "So, we can try and make a dash for it, or remain here."

Adeline shook her head. "You two remain here," she said. "I'm going to make sure the culprit doesn't escape."

She slipped back through the door.

Mary turned to Ian. "I really want to watch," she confessed.

Ian nodded. "Aye, me too," he said. "But it will be hard to explain our presence in the library."

"Do you think they'll search the rest of the library?" Mary asked.

"It's possible," Ian said. "Do you want to call Bradley and warn him?"

Mary slipped into a chair in front of one of the computer stations, and her eyes widened. "Did you know the library has security cameras that can be accessed by this computer?" she said softly, clicking on a mouse.

Ian pulled up another chair and sat next to her. "Well, that makes sense," he said. "If the librarian was in here doing research, she could see the front desk."

Mary nodded, enlarging the screen for the front desk and turning to Ian. "And now we get to watch."

Chapter Thirty-two

The camera feed only displayed in black and white, but it was a clear enough picture that Mary and Ian could see exactly what was going on. The librarian they'd met earlier in the day was behind the circulation desk with her purse in front of her on the counter. She was systematically pulling money out of the drawer and dropping it into her open purse.

"Do you think this is being recorded?" Mary asked.

Ian pulled out his cell phone, opened the camera app, pressed a button and pointed it at the monitor. "It is now," he said.

They watched her walk over to the end of the counter where a donation display had been set up, pick up the bucket and carry it back to her purse. Taking a pair of scissors, she ripped the top off the bucket and turned it upside down over her purse, shaking out all of the bills into her purse.

"She is despicable," Mary said.

"I wonder how often she does this," Ian wondered.

"Look," Mary exclaimed, pointing to a reflection in the window. "It's the policeman."

But they weren't the only ones to catch the reflection. The crooked librarian turned and stared at the door for just a moment, then moved quickly to grab for her purse. But as she jumped forward, the purse moved, just out of her reach. She stared at the purse for a moment, stunned, then moved forward to grab it again. It moved again, noticeably away from the woman.

Her eyes wide, she stepped back, away from her purse, stumbling backwards over the chair next to her. The purse lifted into the air and swung slowly, back and forth, before the woman's face. A moment later, when the police officer entered the library, the librarian ran to him, throwing herself into his arms.

There was no audio, but Ian and Mary could guess what she was saying as she gesticulated wildly in the direction of the purse that now sat quietly on the counter. The policeman moved her away from him and walked over to the counter. He looked at the purse, then pulled out a handful of dollar bills and held them out towards the woman.

Her initial face was one of defiance and shock. Mary could read her lips as she told the officer she had no idea how that money had come to be in her purse. The officer stared at her for a moment, then shrugged and headed towards the door. The woman screamed for the officer, so loudly they could hear it in the back room, but he continued to the door.

Suddenly, the purse was airborne once again, floating towards the woman but out of the sight of the police officer. The woman looked at the purse, then looked at the retreating officer. She yelled something, and he turned around. Nodding her head and pointing to various places behind the desk, Ian and Mary could tell she was finally confessing to the crime.

They sat in the back room watching for another fifteen minutes as backup arrived and the curt librarian was hauled away in a squad car.

When the only person in the view finder was the original police officer, Mary's phone rang. She looked down and then looked at Ian. "It's him," she said. "It's the officer."

She picked up the call. "Hello," she said tentatively.

"Would you please tell Adeline that I appreciate her help?" he asked.

"I would be happy to pass that on," Mary replied. She paused for just a moment. "Um, would it be helpful for you to get an anonymous copy of the security camera recording what happened tonight?"

He chuckled softly and glanced up at the camera. "As long as you edit the Adeline parts out, it would be very helpful," he said.

"You saw?" Mary asked, surprised.

"It was reflected in the window," he said. "Very persuasive."

Mary laughed. "Yes, it seems that it was," she said.

"Oh, and Mrs. Alden," he added.

Mary was silent for a long moment. "How do you know my name?" she asked.

"Caller ID," he replied.

"Oh, of course," she said. "I'm sorry. Yes. What would you like?"

"Give me at least five minutes before you come out of the back room," he said. "That way I will be two blocks away, and I won't need to detain you tonight."

"You trust us?" she asked.

"If you're working with Adeline, I trust you," he said. "And if you need my help, you have my number."

"Thank you," Mary said. "Thank you very much."

Chapter Thirty-three

Bradley looked down at Clarissa sleeping peacefully in her bed and bent down to tuck her in. Then he turned and quietly turned the audio and video monitor on so he could watch her from the other room. He also adjusted the Rem-Pod, a device that not only measured shifts in the magnetic field but would also detect changes in the ambient temperature of the room.

Mike appeared next to him. "Everything okay?" he asked.

"Could you make sure the Rem-Pod appears in the video feed?" he asked.

"The what?" Mike asked.

Bradley shook his head. "This little doohicky with the blinky lights," he said. "Make sure it shows up on the computer's TV screen downstairs."

"Okay, now you're being a little snarky," Mike said, disappearing and then just as quickly reappearing. "Yes, you can see the little doohicky with the blinky lights on the computer's TV screen."

Bradley shrugged. "You're right," he said. "It did sound snarky."

Mike shook his head. "I get it," he said. "We're all a little on edge. So, now that Clarissa's asleep, I can tell you about my quick visit with Mary and Ian."

"You saw Mary?" Bradley asked, momentarily forgetting to lower his voice.

"Shhhh, big guy," Mike reminded him. "Let's go downstairs and talk. You can sit next to your computer's TV screen."

With a final glance at his sleeping daughter, Bradley quietly slipped out of the room and headed downstairs. The entire living room had been outfitted in electronics, from motion detectors and EMF readers to smoke detectors and security cameras.

He stood in the middle of the room and slowly looked around. "You were right," he said. "Katie Brennan is an electrical genius."

Mike glided over to him. "Did you see this little gem, hidden behind the couch?" he asked.

Bradley shook his head. "No, what's there?"

"A backup power source in case somehow the shadow guy is able to take out the breakers," he said. "We'll still be monitoring him."

"I actually feel secure," Bradley said.

"Good," Mike replied. "Because we need to make the shadow kid think that Mary's here with us and not out investigating with Ian."

"How do we do that?" Bradley said.

"I can take care of the majority of the decoy," he said, "but I need you to act like Mary's here."

"You mean, I should talk to her or something?" he asked.

Mike shook his head. "No, you need to convince yourself that she's here," he said. "You need to play a mind-game with yourself that Mary's upstairs sleeping, or in the shower, or wherever. But in your mind, you need to feel like she's here."

"Why?" Bradley asked, not convinced.

"Well, this is going to sound a little crazy," Mike started.

"Oh, well, not a day has gone by since I met Mary that something hasn't sounded a little crazy," Bradley replied with a smile. "So why should today be any different?"

"We put off different vibes, some people might call it auras, depending on our modes," he said. "Especially when we love someone, our auras kind of connect with each other. So, it's obvious to those of us who read auras when you're lonely, frightened, tired, all of those things."

"And those of you who read auras are…" Bradley asked.

"Spiritual beings," Mike said. "Because your spirit is the part of you that sends out your aura. Just like your face—your mouth and your eyes—communicate feelings to humans, your aura does the same thing to spiritual beings."

"So, if I can fool my aura into thinking Mary is safe and sound and nestled upstairs in bed, it's going to send out positive waves?" Bradley asked.

"Actually colors," Mike said. "Positive colors."

Nodding slowly, Bradley met Mike's eyes. "What color is my aura now?" he asked.

"Pissed off dark red," Mike said with a grin. "You're going to have to work on that."

Bradley took a deep breath and slowly let it out. "Okay," he said, closing his eyes. "Give me a second."

He pictured Mary coming down the stairs in his sweatpants, four times too big for her. He pictured her smiling at him as she grabbed another Christmas cookie.

"Good," Mike said. "Good, you're turning green."

Bradley opened one eye. "Isn't green for jealousy?" he asked.

Mike shook his head. "No, green is for love."

Bradley closed his eyes and thought about loving Mary. He remembered the last time they were upstairs and she was in his arms...

"Whoa, cool it there, big guy," Mike said with a smirk. "You just went from balanced green to passionate red. Let's just keep it at green."

"So you can see my aura, right?" Bradley asked.

Mike nodded.

"Okay, I'll keep thinking my Mary thoughts," he said. "And if I get off kilter, you remind me to get back in place. Deal?"

"Deal," Mike agreed.

"So, if we are having this Mary decoy here," Bradley asked, "does that make Rosie and Stanley safer?"

Shrugging, Mike shook his head. "I don't know," he said. "Katie did say she was going to go over there this evening and help them set up their electronics. But, that's really the best we can do."

"I really hate that they're in danger," Bradley said.

"You offered to let them stay here," Mike reminded him. "When you called them this afternoon."

"Yeah, but maybe I should have been more insistent," Bradley said. "If anything happens to them…"

"They've got just about as much stuff as we do," Mike replied. "And they know not to take any risks. They'll be fine."

Bradley ran his hand through his hair and sighed. "I sure hope we can send this kid packing soon," he said. "I want my family back to normal."

"Yeah, whatever that is," Mike replied.

Chapter Thirty-four

"Whatever this is," Ian said as he read through Dr. Buus' notes, "it's certainly not normal."

Mary sat curled up in a chair across the room from Ian, sipping a cup of tea and looking through the newspaper clippings from the library files. "Not normal as in abnormal or not normal as in paranormal?" she asked, looking up and then took another sip from her cup.

"As in both," Ian replied, closing the folder and leaning back in his chair. "As in this kid was seriously messed up."

"Seriously messed up?" Mary asked. "That's your diagnosis?"

Ian smiled at her and shook his head. "No, I agree with Mark," he said. "This is a textbook case of psychopathic disorder. This young man had no moral compass. He showed no emotion or remorse for what he did to his family."

Mary put her cup down on the little table next to the chair. "None at all?" she asked.

He shook his head. "No. He felt that because they didn't give him the attention he deserved, they deserved to be punished," Ian explained. "When he went downstairs on Christmas morning and did not find the bike he wanted, he was angry. They made him angry, so in his mind, punishment was justified."

"And when he discovered they had purchased the bike for him?" Mary asked. "When he found out he was wrong?"

Ian nodded. "Ah, well then, according to his sessions with Mark, it was their fault for not having it under the tree where he expected it," he said. "There was no sorrow or even acceptance of fault for what he did."

"Did Mark ever see any relationship bonds between Tony and the other residents?" Mary asked. "Did anyone ever touch his heart?"

Ian smiled at her. "Ever the romantic, aren't you?" he replied kindly. "There is a great possibility that he didn't have the ability to do that. There have been some studies that say that psychotic behavior is hard-wired into our brains."

"Born evil," Mary replied.

"Well, not necessarily evil," Ian said. "There are plenty of high-functioning psychopaths out there who lead very full and satisfying lives. Psychopaths are charming, although it's superficial. They are generally quite smart and articulate. And, because they feel no remorse, guilt or anxiety, they display an inordinate amount of confidence in themselves and their actions."

"So, they use their traits for good?" Mary asked.

"For their own good," Ian replied. "They are always aware of what's best for them. They tend to be narcissistic, manipulative, and never feel bad about their actions."

"Sounds scary," Mary said.

Ian shrugged. "Or useful, depending on your point of view," he said. "Ian Fleming, the author of the James Bond series, modeled James Bond after a British World War II spy who had very strong, successful, psychopathic tendencies."

"Then what differentiates successful and criminal psychopaths?" she asked.

"Well, that's the kicker," Ian said. "We don't know. It could be environment. It could be other personality traits, or it could be something we haven't discovered yet. But there is something quite interesting in a lot of the studies."

Ian sat forward and clasped his hands together. "They have found many cases where psychopaths, especially criminal psychopaths, felt they were led or guided by a voice."

Mary's eyes widened. "Paranormal influence?" she asked.

He smiled and nodded. "Aye, well that's probably an avenue they didn't investigate," he said, "seeing as most of the analysts don't believe in the paranormal."

"But you believe…" she began.

"Aye, as I've studied criminology and the paranormal, there are some connections between influence on weaker minds and, let's just say, paranormal entities," he said. "But I don't have enough data on psychopaths."

She picked up her tea and sipped again, her mind racing as she thought about the implications of Ian's words. "So, are you saying that Tony might have been influenced to do what he did?" she asked.

"Do you believe people are born evil?" he asked, answering her question with one of his own.

She shook her head. "No, I don't," she said. "But I believe that they can be born with tendencies to do evil. They just have to choose which way they want to go."

He met her eyes and remained silent for a moment. "Or they're guided."

Chapter Thirty-five

"I don't think I care for all these highfalutin electronic devices hanging around our house," Stanley said, eyeing the various instruments with disdain. "Ain't no guarantee that they won't set the house on fire themselves."

Rosie looked up from her novel and shook her head. "Stanley, we promised Bradley that we would keep them on until they've dealt with the shadow thing," she said. "And if you don't want to do that, well then, we can always spend the night at Mary's house."

Stanley grumbled, got up from the recliner and walked across the room to Rosie. "I ain't no girly-girl having to have an overnighter 'cause I'm scared of some shadow," he said. "We ain't had nothing bother us afore, and we've been working with Mary longer than Bradley has."

"Well, that's true," Rosie agreed. "But this one is different. This one hasn't come to get help. This one seems like it just wants to start trouble."

"I ain't never been afraid of trouble," he said.

Rosie sighed and put her book down on the couch. "Stanley, you know that I have the utmost confidence in your bravery and your abilities," she said. "Don't you?"

Stanley shrugged and nodded. "I s'pose so."

"Good," she immediately replied. "Because I don't want you to do anything that would endanger your life. You don't need to be a hero; you just need to stay safe."

Stanley walked away from her and started to pace across the room. "The way I see it," he began, "is that maybe someone oughta face that whippersnapper down. It ain't nothing but a kid ghost. All it needs is a firm hand, some discipline, that's all."

"No, Stanley," Rosie said firmly. "It's not just a kid ghost. It's as old as we are, and it's powerful enough to have frightened Mary."

He shook his head. "Awww, she was just scared 'cause of her condition," he countered. "Iffen she wasn't carrying a baby, she would have taken it out the first time."

"We don't know that," Rosie said. "We can't see it or feel it like she does. We need to take her word for it."

Stanley stopped pacing and looked down at Rosie. "Fine," he said. "Is that what you want me to say? Okay, I said it. Fine."

She stood up, walked over to him and slipped her hands around his waist, laying her head against his shoulder. "No, I want you to say that you will not do anything that will endanger the love of my life," she whispered. "Because if something were to happen to you, I don't think I could survive it."

He sighed, and she could feel the anger and frustration leave his body. Then he wrapped his arms around her and just held her. "I s'pose I feel the same way about you," he said. "That's why it's so goldurn frustrating to think something might be threatening you and I can't do a dang thing about it."

"Something is threatening both of us," she reminded him. "And we are doing something. We are protecting ourselves."

"We're hiding like cowards," he grumbled.

She pulled away slightly and looked up at him. "Stanley," she said sharply.

"I ain't saying I'm gonna do anything else," he quickly countered. "I'm just saying I'm feeling like a wimp."

"He that fights and runs away lives to fight another day," Rosie quoted to him.

"Well, I ain't running away," Stanley exclaimed. "That's for sure."

"I didn't mean that you are running away," she replied, exasperated. "I only meant that it is sometimes wiser to wait for the right opportunity to fight, rather than rush in without knowledge or defenses."

"Well, and how's we gonna get knowledge unless we face it?" he argued.

"We wait until Ian…" she began.

Stanley quickly put a hand over her mouth and glanced around the room. "You 'member what Bradley told us tonight?" he asked, nodding meaningfully at her.

Her eyes wide, she nodded back, and he removed his hand.

"I mean, isn't it nice that Mary's at home," she said loudly. "Safe and sound in her bedroom."

Stanley glanced slowly around the room. "Speaking of bedroom," he said, "I'm thinking it's time to retire for the night. You go wash up and I'll lock up."

Rosie nodded. "Okay," she replied, her voice a little shaky. "I'll go wash up."

Chapter Thirty-six

Stanley sat at the edge of the bed in the guestroom, waiting in the darkness, watching the flashing display lights reflecting on the hallway wall. His iPhone in his hand, he looked down at the time. It had been thirty minutes since Rosie had kissed him goodnight and headed to their bedroom. She had to be asleep. He stood up and walked to the doorway, listening intently until he heard the soft, rhythmic breathing of his sweetheart.

"'Bout time she fell asleep," he muttered.

He walked back, sat on the edge of the bed and flipped through the pages of apps he had. Finally he came to the one he wanted. It was a ghost detector. The description said that it guaranteed that he would be able to communicate with ghosts in his house.

"Don't need none of them fancy electronics," he said, engaging the app. "I'll show them what I can do."

The screen glowed as a neon-green radar appeared on the black background. An indicator arm circulated around the interior of the radar screen, searching for paranormal phenomena. "Come on," Stanley whispered. "I paid good money for you. You better work."

Suddenly an electronic voice read out, "Robert."

"Robert?" Stanley asked his phone. "Is that your name?"

The voice replied again. "Texas."

"Texas?" Stanley asked. "I thought you were from Wisconsin. Were you born in Texas?"

"Pancakes."

Stanley moved the phone away from him and stared. "What the hell does pancakes have to do with this?" he asked. "You hungry, boy?"

Stanley waited for another response, but minutes went by with the last response, pancakes, still displayed at the top of the screen.

"Ain't you talking to me until I make you pancakes?" he asked quietly.

"Applause."

"Does that mean I'm right?" Stanley asked. "Does that mean you're clapping 'cause I figgered it out?"

The radar screen was still searching, but nothing else was happening. He stared down at the phone. "The description had over one thousand five-star reviews," he whispered. "Can't all those folks be lying."

He stared at the screen for a few more moments.

"Feed," it exclaimed.

"Fine," Stanley huffed. "I'll make you pancakes."

He pulled his robe on over his pajamas and carefully snuck out of the guest room. The display lights were still gently flickering, indicating that they weren't picking up any paranormal activity. Stanley scoffed in their direction. "Highfalutin, fancy-schmancy instruments," he whispered. "You ain't got nothing on my ghost detector."

Tip-toeing across the room, he went to the cupboard where Rosie kept the pancake mix. Placing his phone on the counter, he poured about two cups of dry mix into a bowl and then turned to get the eggs from the refrigerator. As he turned, the phone exclaimed, "newspaper."

"Whatcha want in the newspaper?" he asked.

"Height."

"What?" Stanley asked, walking back.

"Grandmother."

"I ain't no one's grandmother," Stanley said. "Now do you want pancakes or dontcha?"

"Hamburger."

"Why can't you make up your mind?" Stanley exclaimed.

"Stanley, what's wrong?" Rosie asked, wiping the sleep out of her eyes. "Why are you in the kitchen? And who were you talking to?"

Stanley slid a kitchen towel over the phone and smiled at Rosie. "Well, I was a mite hungry," he said. "And I was thinking about making myself a little late-night snack. But then I disremembered I get terrible heartburn when I do that."

Rosie nodded. "Yes, you do," she said. "You shouldn't eat after ten."

He came around the counter and put his hand over her shoulders, guiding her back towards her bedroom. "I'm so sorry I woke you," he said gently. "Let me tuck you back in."

Once they were out of hearing distance, the app responded again.

"Fire."

"Death."

Chapter Thirty-seven

Adeline glided through the room and perched herself on the edge of the other occasional chair in the room. "You know, I was always a great fan of mysteries," she said. "But one of my most annoying traits was that I always solved them before the end of the book."

Mary smiled at her. "I wouldn't call that annoying," she said. "I would call that genius."

"Well, that's nice of you to say," Adeline replied. "But as someone who always had to finish a book once she started it, it really made for a very tedious ending."

"It would seem you have a natural talent for mystery solving," Ian said. "And, I must admit, there are things about this Tony Lancaster case that have me quite at wits end. You seem to have researched him more than most. What did you discover?"

"I was hoping you'd ask," Adeline admitted, scooting back in the chair and relaxing, "for I have wanted to share my suppositions with others to see whether or not they were viable."

Ian nodded. "First supposition?" he asked.

"Well, in one file you will find that I collected clippings from all of the deaths at the asylum from the year Tony was imprisoned to the year they closed the asylum," she said.

"Why didn't you stop once Tony died?" Mary asked.

Adeline smiled at her. "Now, see, that's where the first supposition comes in," she said. "Many of the deaths were natural causes, but a handful were because of spontaneous fires."

"Including Dr. Mark Buus," Ian inserted.

"Exactly so," Adeline agreed. "Isn't it odd that a building built out of brick and cinder block would have so many strange and unexplained fires?"

Mary nodded. "I suppose it is," she agreed.

"And, furthermore," Adeline continued, "isn't it odd that everyone who died from a fire in the asylum had a connection of some sort to Tony Lancaster?"

Mary sat up. "Really?" she asked.

Adeline nodded slowly. "Yes, I did as much collaborative fact checking as I could," she said. "But there is definitely a connection between Tony and at least most of the fires."

"And, now that we have Mark's files," Ian said, "perhaps we can even ascertain a more solid link." He looked over at Mary. "Do you have the file about the deaths?"

Mary flipped through the files in her lap and finally pulled one free. "Here it is," she said with a smile in Adeline's direction, "in perfect chronological order."

"Of course," Adeline said. "Much easier to find that way."

"Okay," Ian said, looking through Dr. Buus's files. "Give me the first name on the list."

Mary pulled out the first paperclipped item. It contained an obituary and several articles from the local paper, as well as an article from the Madison paper. "Frank Marnette."

Ian glanced down the paperwork. "Okay, we have a match," he said. "Tony complained that Frank Marnette, the resident whose room was next door to his, annoyed him. Frank would constantly call over to Tony's room and want to speak with him."

"That's annoying?" Mary asked.

"To Tony it was," Ian replied. "Tony told Mark that someday he was going to kill Frank because someone that annoying had no place on earth."

"Well, that's disturbing," Mary said.

"And even more interesting is this," Ian added. "Tony said the best way to kill people was with fire because it was like the pastor at his church once said, from dust you came and to dust you will return."

"He listened to the words of his pastor?" Adeline asked. "Is that unusual? He didn't seem to be the religious type at all."

"He might not have been religious," Mary mused thoughtfully, "only worshipful."

Ian glanced over at her. "Okay, interesting premise," he said. "Explain."

She nodded. "So, psychopaths are all about placing themselves in the best positions of, for lack of a better word, power," Mary explained. "They are looking out for themselves, and they like feeling in control over others."

"Okay, I'm with you so far," Ian said.

"Picture a young boy going to a church with his family," Mary said. "There in the front of the church, telling everyone what to do, putting, excuse the pun, the fear of God in everyone, is the pastor. He is the guy in control. He is the one with the power. He is the one that gets to call the shots. A burgeoning psychopath could look upon a person like that and want to model himself after him."

"Cleansed by fire," Ian said slowly.

"To lay your life down for a greater cause," Adeline added.

"I will come again in glory to rule the world," Mary added softly.

Chapter Thirty-eight

Bradley slowly crept down the stairs, keeping his weight against the wall, so the steps didn't creak. He scanned the room, noting the flickering lights of all the devices Katie had helped him set up. They were all still in normal mode. Nothing paranormal had disturbed them. He should feel relaxed, at ease, but there was something…

Stopping at the bottom of the stairs he waited as the hairs on the back of his neck stood at attention. There was something else in the house, something just on the edge of consciousness. It was something that pulled at him. The air was heavier. The atmosphere tingled. And he had the distinct feeling he was being watched.

He closed his eyes, just for a moment to shut out all of the distractions, and listened. Listened with his ears and with his intuition. He turned slowly and opened his eyes. The kitchen, he decided. Whatever it was, it came from the kitchen.

He thought for a moment about contacting Mike. He had actually stepped back towards the staircase when he saw it move. He countered, moving quickly across the living room floor to the edge of the kitchen. Back pressed against the wall, he had a quick flashback to the first night he'd stayed in Mary's house, the first night he'd actually encountered a ghost, the first night he realized there was much more to this life than what you could see and feel. But this was not Earl, the loud and clumsy, headless soldier looking for his final resting spot. No, this was something far more deft and evasive.

He slid around the corner into the kitchen and, at the edge of his sight, caught movement in the far corner of the kitchen. Wasn't that where Mary had first seen the shadowed entity?

All pretense of concealment gone, Bradley flew through the kitchen towards the back door. But when he reached the wall, nothing was there.

"Of course nothing's here," he muttered, leaning against the wall and running his hand through his hair. "It was a ghost."

"Where was a ghost?" Mike asked, appearing in the middle of the kitchen.

Pushing himself away from the wall, Bradley sent Mike a look of disgust. "Great help you are," he muttered, walking past the guardian angel.

"What?" Mike exclaimed, following after him. "What?"

"I just came down here and saw a shadow in the kitchen," Bradley said accusingly.

"Are you sure?" Mike asked angrily.

Bradley turned around and went nose to nose with Mike. "Am I sure?" he demanded. "I'm a trained professional. I know what I saw, and I saw a shadow lurking in the kitchen."

"Oh, so now it was lurking," Mike replied. "Did any of the monitors go off?"

Bradley shook his head. "No, they didn't," he said. "But they're machines, not angels."

He turned from Mike, marched to the couch, and began tossing the throw pillows over to one corner.

"What are you doing?" Mike asked.

Bradley sat down on the couch and pulled the throw over his shoulder. "Well, since I can't trust your abilities to protect my family, I guess I'm going to stay on the couch tonight."

"Listen to me, Mr. Trained Professional." Mike countered. "Nothing evil, malignant or threatening entered this house tonight. I would have known."

Bradley started to speak, then stopped and sniffed the air. "Do you smell that?" he asked.

"I'm an angel," Mike snapped. "I can't smell things anymore, or didn't they explain that in trained professional school?"

Bradley smiled sheepishly and nodded. "Hey, I'm sorry," he said and took another deep breath of the air. "That was totally uncalled for. Boy, I wish you could smell it. It's like…"

"What?" Mike asked, suddenly suspicious.

Bradley yawned widely and smiled. "So. Nothing evil was in the house?" he asked.

Mike shook his head. "No, nothing evil," he said. "But there could have been another random spirit just wandering through."

Nodding, Bradley sat down and leaned back against the couch. "Okay, well, that makes total sense," he said. "It was probably someone looking for Mary for help. I'm really sorry, Mike. I was a total jerk."

Mike looked down on Bradley. "What does it smell like?" he asked.

Bradley inhaled deeply, his face relaxing and his smile widening. "Like gingerbread cookies and…" He sniffed again. "Pine trees."

"Isn't that what Mary smelled last night?" Mike asked.

Bradley yawned again, got up and started to walk towards the stairs.

"Where are you going?" Mike demanded.

Bradley looked over his shoulder and shrugged. "To bed," he said. "Suddenly, I'm really tired."

"But I thought you were going to sleep down here because you were worried," Mike replied.

Bradley yawned again. "No," he said. "I'm good. If it was anything bad, you would have known."

His mouth opened in astonishment, Mike watched Bradley casually walk back up the stairs. Finally, when he heard the bedroom door close, he shook his head in disbelief. "I so don't understand what just happened," he said, slowly scanning the room. "And I don't like it one bit. Not one little bit."

Chapter Thirty-nine

Stanley's head slipped forward, and with a start, he shook himself, trying once again to evade the sleep that had been trying to take him over for hours. He was seated on the couch, facing the Christmas tree, trying to keep a vigilant watch over his home and, most importantly, his dear wife.

He glanced at the clock on the wall. It was nearly 4:00 AM. He wondered vaguely about how late ghosts stay up haunting a house. His eyes started to close again, and he fought the exhaustion. "I gotta stay up," he said aloud. "Gotta protect the house."

Suddenly an overpowering scent seemed to surround him. He inhaled it and, feeling revitalized, inhaled it again. It smelled like someone had opened a window to a pine forest on a cold winter's day. The sharpness of the pine needles and the coolness of the air pushed the exhaustion away.

Stanley stood up and looked around the room, trying to place where the smell was coming from. He walked over to the door to make sure there wasn't a leak somewhere that would need to be insulated. But the door was tight, no air seeping through.

Walking over to the shelves where Rosie displayed a number of candles, he picked up each candle and sniffed. "Nothing but perfumey stuff in here," he muttered as he went through several candles and didn't find what he was looking for.

Finally, he went into the kitchen to sniff around in there. He could smell the fragrance of the dishwashing soap and the counter cleaner, but nothing like the smell he'd encountered in the living room.

He turned and, with a shrug, went back to the couch. The scent wasn't quite as strong as earlier, but it still lingered in the room. He was about to sit back on the couch when he noticed a DVD sitting on the coffee table. The old, black and white, action movie was one of his favorites, and even though he'd seen it more than a dozen times, it always kept him on the edge of his seat.

He picked it up and stared at it for a moment. He hadn't watched the movie for several years, maybe even five or six years. Last he recalled, the movie was in a box of old DVDs he'd put down in the basement just before he'd married Rosie. How in the world did it get upstairs?

Shrugging, he crossed the room, stuck the movie into the DVD player and settled himself in for two hours of pure enjoyment.

As Stanley's attention was drawn to the television screen, a shadowed figure paused next to the Christmas tree behind him. It froze for a long moment, then slowly faded away.

Chapter Forty

"Good morning."

Mary sat up quickly and saw Mike sitting in the small chair in her bedroom.

"Mike! Is everything okay?" she asked frantically. "Bradley? Clarissa?"

"They're fine," he said quickly. "Sorry, I didn't mean to scare you. They are just fine. Bradley is driving Clarissa to school for an early meeting, so I thought I'd take a minute to talk to you."

Mary glanced over at the clock on the nightstand. It was 7:30, and she sighed in relief. "I thought it was much later," she said. "We stayed up until about two talking about the information we found." She met his eyes. "This is unlike anything I've ever faced before."

Mike nodded. "I know," he said. "And I'm trying to get more help because I think we're going to need it."

"That doesn't make me feel much better," she admitted. "I really don't like it when you're worried."

"Well, I am, so be careful," he said. "Be very careful."

He was silent for a few moments, and Mary studied him. "So?" she finally asked.

"What?" he asked, trying to act innocent.

"You would not have come here just to tell me to be careful," she said. "You already said that last night. So…what?"

He stood up and slowly glided back and forth. Then he stopped and sighed. "It's probably nothing," he began.

"Then it will be no big deal if you tell me," she urged.

"Remember the first night?" he asked. "When you came downstairs and saw the shadow in the kitchen?"

Mary nodded. "It's a little fuzzy for some reason," she said. "But I do remember it."

"Okay, you said you smelled something," he prompted.

Her eyes widened. "That's right," she said slowly. "It smelled like vanilla and…" She stopped and concentrated for a moment. "Pine trees. It smelled like pine trees."

"And even though you were a little freaked about seeing another shadow in the house, what did you do?" he asked.

She looked at him in disbelief. "I went to bed," she said slowly. "I turned around and went to bed."

"And slept like a rock as I recall," he said with a slight smile.

"Not just me," she reminded him. "Bradley slept right through Ian knocking on the door."

"Which is highly unlike the big guy," Mike said.

"Totally unlike him," she agreed. "He's a very light sleeper—especially when he thinks we're being threatened."

"So, last night I came downstairs to find Bradley in the kitchen, pretty worked up because he saw a shadow in there and none of the electronics had detected anything," Mike said.

"Nothing picked it up?" she asked.

He shook his head. "And, I didn't even sense it," he admitted. "And he was not too happy with me."

"He didn't get upset with you, did he?" she asked.

"It was fine," Mike said. "I would have done the same thing if I had been in his shoes." Then he stopped for a moment and studied Mary. "Okay, let's be honest here. The big guy was majorly pissed at

194

me, at the electronics, at the whole situation. It was more a frustrated anger than anything else. And, like I said, I get it, totally."

"Then what happened?" Mary asked.

Mike smiled and nodded. "Then he smelled something," he said. "He asked me if I could smell it, and I explained that I didn't come with a working sense of smell anymore. But he was even oblivious to my sparkly wit. He just kept sniffing the air and smiling. The anger was gone. The worry was gone. He apologized to me and then…"

"Then?" Mary repeated.

"Then he went to bed," Mike said, perplexed. "After saying that he couldn't trust any of the warning systems in the house, he just went to bed."

"He didn't say he didn't trust you, did he?" Mary asked.

"Well, he was upset that I didn't catch on that there was a bogey in the house," Mike admitted. "And I don't know why I didn't catch it either. Flew right in under the radar."

"And then started crop dusting the 'feel good and go to bed' spray," she added. "Right?"

"Right," he agreed, nodding. "I'd like to explain it, but I've got nothing."

"Do you think it's Tony?" she asked.

"Tony?"

"Oh, okay. Sorry. Time to catch you up," she said. "Tony Lancaster is the name of the boy who burnt the house down around his parents, who went to the asylum, who committed suicide there and then, somehow, was able to come back and burn up the people he didn't really care for."

Mike stared at her for a long moment. "Holy crap," he finally said. "That kid's messed up!"

"Yeah," Mary agreed. "Tell me about it. But, more to the point, do you think Tony has the ability to disarm people, let them think there's no problems and then attack?"

Mike thought about it for a moment and then shook his head. "The first time…Tony, right?" he asked. Mary nodded.

"Okay, the first time Tony was in the house," Mike continued, "I felt him. I felt him even before you called to me. I knew something threatening was on the premises." He stopped for a moment and considered a few things. "Actually, I think I got a whiff of the threatening earlier in the evening when we were in the kitchen and you thought you saw something."

Mary nodded. "And he disappeared before you could zone in on anything substantial."

"Right," Mike agreed. "Right. So, the spidey-sense is working for threatening spirits. And last night, I didn't feel any threatening feelings at all."

"So, we've got another shadowy spirit hanging around the house?" Mary asked.

"Looks like," Mike replied.

"Never a dull moment," Mary said with a sigh, and then she smiled at him.

Mike grinned. "Well, you knew the job was dangerous when you took it."

Her smile faltered, and she shook her head. "Not this dangerous," she said, placing her hands protectively on her stomach. "Not this dangerous."

Chapter Forty-one

The house was bright with morning sun when Rosie left her bedroom the next morning. Slipping on her robe as she walked down the hallway, she stopped, and her heart dropped when she saw Stanley sprawled out on the couch. She rushed over, fearing the worst, and laid her hand on his chest to listen for his heartbeat. With a sigh of relief, she held her hand over the strong beat of his heart.

"Oh, Stanley," she whispered. "You scared me to death."

Her soft words were not intended to wake her slumbering husband, but a moment later his eyes fluttered open. It took him only another moment to realize where he was. "Must have finally dozed off," he mumbled. "What time is it anyhow?"

"It's about 7:30," Rosie replied. "How late did you stay up?"

"Well, I ain't saying I stayed up, and I ain't saying I didn't," he said. "All you need to know is the house was safe and sound."

Leaning forward, she placed a gentle kiss on his lips. "Thank you, Stanley," she said. "I know you watched over me so I wouldn't have to worry."

He blushed slightly. "It's what I'm s'posed to do," he said.

"Well, why don't you go back into our bedroom and take a nap," she suggested. "I was just going to do some Christmas baking this morning, so there's no place we need to go."

He stood up and wobbled a little on his feet. "You sure?" he asked. "I'm barely tired at all."

"I'm sure," she said, holding back a smile. "And maybe later this afternoon we can go by and see Bradley and Clarissa."

"Good idea," Stanley said, covering a yawn. "We need a little meeting with them, compare notes and all."

"Yes, I know that Bradley will want to hear about your experiences," she assured him.

"Okay then," he nodded. "I'll just close my eyes for a few minutes."

"You do that," she said. "And I'll keep myself busy in the kitchen."

Rosie watched Stanley walk down the hall, half asleep, towards their bedroom with a loving smile on her face. "Staying up all night to protect me," she whispered. "What a wonderful man."

Twenty minutes later, Rosie was elbows deep in sugar cookie dough, forming it into separate rounds to refrigerate for a few hours. Then she'd be able to roll them out and cut them into shapes. She glanced over to the calendar on the wall. Christmas was less than a week away. Would they be safe by then? Or would their Christmas be overshadowed with fear?

She lifted one of the rounds of dough out of the bowl and placed it on the piece of plastic wrap she had waiting on the counter. Tightly wrapping the dough up, she turned towards the refrigerator and froze. The dough dropped from her nerveless hands as she read the words printed in block letters on the white board attached to the side of the fridge.

"FIRE"

"BURN"

Chapter Forty-two

Rosie opened the door before Bradley could knock and placed her finger over her lips for silence. Then she let him inside and led him into the kitchen.

"Stanley was up all night," she whispered once they were in the kitchen. "And I don't want to wake him for anything."

Bradley nodded. "Did any of your electronics go off last night?" he asked softly.

She shook her head. "Not that I know of," she replied. "But, for some reason, Stanley stayed out in the living room all night. I found him in the recliner this morning. 'Bout scared me to death. I thought he wasn't breathing."

"Did he say anything?"

"No, but I'm sure it was because he didn't want me to worry," she replied, and then she pointed to the white board. "But this certainly caught my attention."

Bradley inhaled sharply when he read the words. "I think you two ought to think about staying at our house tonight," he said. "This is getting—"

"I ain't staying at no one else's house but my own," Stanley said, his hands on his hips. "We got the situation well in hand."

"Stanley, I'm so sorry," Rosie said. "I didn't mean to wake you."

"I woke up when I heard the front door open," he replied, accusing her with his gaze. "I got the ears of a hawk."

"I was just so afraid," Rosie began. "I didn't..."

"You were afraid, so you called Bradley and didn't wake me up?" he asked, his voice filled with hurt. "I told you I'd protect you, Rosie. I promised you I would."

"No! No, it wasn't like that at all," Rosie pleaded. "I wanted you to sleep because you stayed up all night."

"Stayed up protecting you and our home," he said, glaring at her. "And I did a goldurn good job at it, too."

"Yes, you did," Rosie replied. "You did a—"

"Then why did you have to call someone else when you was scared?" he asked angrily.

"Stanley..." she began.

"Stanley, did you see these last night?" Bradley asked, interrupting their argument and pointing to the words on the board.

The fight went out of him, and Stanley stared in disbelief. "No," he said softly. "No, I didn't."

"What happened last night that made you decide to stay up?" Bradley asked, his voice firm and professional.

"I saw something," he said. "Something on my ghost finder app."

"Your what?" Rosie asked.

"My ghost finder app," he exclaimed. "It's made to detect paranormal activity in your house. Even has a voice readout when the ghost is trying to talk to you."

Bradley sighed. "Stanley, those things are nonsense," he said. "They can't really tell you the words ghosts are saying. Mary's even done tests with them. They just don't work."

Stanley lifted his head just a little higher and met Bradley's eyes. "Don't you think I knowed that?" he asked. "Don't you think after the first couple o' nonsense words I figured it out?"

His eyes narrowed, and he took a deep breath. "But then after I walked Rosie back to bed last night, I come back here to the kitchen to get my phone and get myself back in bed. What do I find? The last two entries on the voice app. Fire and death."

"Oh my!" Rosie exclaimed.

But Stanley didn't look in her direction. He kept his gaze locked with Bradley's. "I knewed that ghost was playing with us," he said. "And I knewed it had manipulated the phone app."

Bradley nodded. "You're exactly right, Stanley," he said. "It had."

"And I knewed I had to stay up all night to keep what's mine safe," he said.

"And you did just that," Bradley replied.

"Yes I did," Stanley replied. "And words on a white board or no, I intend to do it again tonight."

Chapter Forty-three

Ian was in the tiny kitchen of the cottage when Mary came out of her bedroom dressed and ready for the day. He looked over his shoulder at her as he stirred a pan of scrambled eggs. "Sleep well?" he asked.

She nodded and took a cup out of the cupboard for tea. "Yes, really well," she said. "And when I woke up, there was an angel standing next to my bed."

Grinning, Ian picked up the kettle and added hot water after Mary had dropped a bag of herbal tea into her cup. "Mike came by to check on you?" he asked.

Nodding her thanks, she picked up the paper tag and dipped the soaked tea bag up and down in the water. "Not just check in, but report in," she said. "They had another encounter with the second shadowy figure."

"The second one?" Ian asked, confused.

"The one that seems to be associated with some kind of scent that relaxes you," she said.

"Ah, the one that made you sleep in the first morning," he said, nodding. "And what was the result this time?"

"It turned Bradley from frantically concerned to intensely laid back," Mary said.

Ian scooped the eggs onto two plates, added toast and bacon and carried them to the little table situated in a sunny nook. "Does that concern you?" he asked.

She picked up a piece of bacon, took a bite and smiled gratefully. "Thanks for breakfast," she said, and he nodded in response. "It only concerns me if there is real trouble that's being masked."

"You mean Tony is using it," he said.

"Exactly," Mary replied. "Is it a ruse to have everyone sleeping so soundly…"

She stopped and shook her head. "I don't even want to say it," she said.

Suddenly Adeline appeared in the extra seat at the table. "Good morning," she said brightly. "And how did you both sleep?"

"Very well," Mary said. "Thank you. The bed was so comfortable."

Adeline turned to Ian. "And you?"

"Aye, fine," he said with a nod. "It was a fine bed"

"And you didn't sleep a wink," she said, meeting his eyes. "A fine bed isn't going to cure your sleep. But we can talk about that later."

She turned to Mary. "Tell me about your ability," she said. "How you work with ghosts."

"Well, I don't really know how it works," Mary said. "But ghosts are, for lack of a better word, attracted to me. They know I can help them move from their current state onto the next state."

"So, they are in a kind of limbo," Adeline surmised. "A place where they do the same things over and over again? Or are stuck in the same place? Correct?"

"Yes. Exactly," Mary said. "And once they interact with me, they become kind of attached, so they can move away from where they were and find me so I can help them."

"And if I were a ghost stuck in an asylum," Adeline said, "you might be the key to my breakout."

Mary sat back in her chair. "I guess I hadn't thought of that before," she said slowly. "When we had our first interaction at the asylum, it was probably enough for him to connect."

"And, by using whatever magnetic force you possess, he could free himself from the chains of his prison," Adeline finished.

"It makes perfect sense," Ian agreed. "But what held him at the asylum? It seems that he had the ability to come and go as he pleased if you agree that the deaths caused by fire over the years were his doing."

Adeline nodded. "Oh, I think we all agree that's a very high probability," she said. "But I never connected any other deaths, outside the asylum, to Tony. No one he knew in town or through school died in a fire."

"So, he only had power in the asylum," Mary said.

"Or he only had a portal into the asylum," Adeline countered.

"That's an interesting idea," Ian said. "And how do you suggest we test your hypothesis?"

Adeline smiled at him. "Why, we must all go back to the asylum and find out for ourselves."

Chapter Forty-four

Once the chain was removed from around the handles, the doors opened easily and without much ado. The light reflecting off the snow-covered fields around the asylum shone through the nooks and crannies of the boards that covered the windows, dimly lighting the interior of the building.

Ian walked into the front lobby first and then turned to Mary to guide her away from potential stumbling risks. They stood together in the middle of the lobby, Adeline at their side, and took a moment to ascertain the atmosphere of the building.

"Not exactly inviting," Mary said. "But much better than the first time."

Ian nodded. "Aye, it's a sad place with horrible memories locked up inside," he agreed. "But nothing malevolent."

"Should we try Tony's old room?" Mary asked.

"Seems the best place to start," Ian agreed.

"How do you know which one is his room?" Adeline asked.

"It was in his records," Ian explained. "The ones that Dr. Buus gave us."

Suddenly, Mark Buus appeared in front of them. "You came back?" he asked, surprised. "This isn't a very safe place to visit."

"We still have some questions to be answered," Ian said. "And, if possible, we'd like to go directly to the source."

"Which source?" Dr. Buus asked.

"Perhaps the people who died in the fires after Tony committed suicide," Mary suggested. "Are any of them still here?"

Dr. Buus shrugged. "I don't know," he said. "I tend to stay near my office. But I can show you their rooms."

Dr. Buus turned and glided towards one of the hallways, and they began to follow before Mary noticed that Adeline was still standing in the center of the lobby. "Adeline? Mary questioned.

Adeline was standing still, staring at Dr. Buus.

Mary moved closer. "Adeline?" she asked again.

Finally, Adeline slowly turned to Mary. "Mary," she whispered. "He's a ghost."

Mary grinned. "Yes, he is," she said. "And remember, so are you."

Adeline looked surprised for a moment and then chuckled. "Why, so I am," she said. "I suppose I forgot."

"Well, that's certainly understandable," Mary said. "Shall we go?"

"Oh, of course," Adeline agreed.

They quickly caught up with Ian and then headed down the corridor after the doctor. They came to a T in the hall, and the doctor led them to the left. This hall was narrower, and the metal doors were every six feet. Instead of a window, the doors had a small opening with bars. As they walked past a room with an open door, Mary looked in. They were like prison cells with a metal bunk, a toilet, a sink and a small table and chair.

"These are so bare," Mary said.

Dr. Buus looked over his shoulder at her. "Well, this was a prison for the most part," he said. "And those who hadn't committed crimes were here because their families couldn't take care of them or they couldn't take care of themselves."

"This is so sad," she replied.

He nodded. "Yes, it is," he said. "And frustrating for those of us who came here to help." He shook his head. "There was always too much work and not enough time. I don't know if I ever made a difference in any of their lives."

He stopped at one of the doors. "This was Jody's room," he said sadly. "Jody Simmons. She was the sweetest little girl."

"Why was she here?" Ian asked.

"Her family, on advice from a doctor, placed her in here because she had mental problems," Dr. Buus said.

"What kind of mental problems?" Ian asked.

"Poor social interaction skills, poor verbal skills, she would stare out into space for long periods of time," Dr. Buus said. "She didn't interact at all with her family. She would just sit in a room by herself and rock."

"Sounds like autism," Mary said.

Dr. Buus nodded. "Yes. Yes, that's what we thought, too," he agreed. "Autism. But, I couldn't allow them to treat her. She was just too tiny and sweet."

"Treat her?" Mary asked.

"Yes, for autistic children the recommendation in my time was medication and electric shock treatment," he said. "The medication was LSD, and the side-effects were awful."

"That's criminal," Mary replied, repulsed.

He nodded. "That's what I thought, too," he said. "And the behavioral change treatments were things I wouldn't have used on an animal. The primary emphasis was on punishment and pain."

"A child can't respond to anything like that," Mary said.

"Unfortunately," Ian inserted, "medical science knew very little about autism. They actually linked it with schizophrenia. It wasn't until the 1980s and 1990s that they finally discovered the benefits of controlled learning environments and other types of therapy."

"She loved music," Dr. Buss said.

"I beg your pardon?" Mary said.

He smiled at her. "Jody loved music," he said. "When I brought in a music box, she would smile. It was such a breakthrough. I thought that if we could continue using music and positive reinforcement she might actually be able to return to her home."

"What happened?" Ian asked.

Dr. Buus sighed sadly. "She died," he said, his voice breaking. "She died in a fire."

Chapter Forty-five

"Why would he want to kill her?" Mary asked. "Jody was harmless."

Dr. Buus shook his head. "She was sweet. She was innocent. And she was weaker than he was," he explained. "That was all the motivation he needed."

Mary stepped into the tiny room and gasped softly when the child appeared in the corner of the room. "Hello, Jody," Mary said softly.

"She's in there?" Dr. Buus asked, sliding through the wall and entering the room.

As soon as she saw the doctor, the child's face filled with joy. The doctor glided across the room and knelt in front of her. "Oh, it's so good to see you," he said, emotion thick in his voice. "How are you?"

She patted her ear and then looked at him expectantly.

"Music?" he asked. "You want music?"

She smiled again and patted her ear.

Dr. Buus turned to Ian and Mary, in dismay. "I don't have any music," he said, pleading for help.

Ian pulled out his cell phone and touched a music app. In moments, a soft lullaby filled the room, echoing off the bare and paint-chipped walls. The child's smile grew wider, and she put her tiny hand on the shoulder of the doctor. Reverently, she leaned forward and placed a kiss on his cheek.

Crystalline tears trickled down the doctor's face as he smiled back at the child. But then, the look on his face turned to confusion.

"What's wrong?" Ian asked.

"There's a large, glowing white light in the corner of this room," he said. "And I know it wasn't there before."

Mary smiled over at Ian, tears forming in her eyes. "Does Jody see it?"

Dr. Buus motioned to Jody to look, and the child's eyes opened in wonder when she looked in the direction her trusted friend pointed.

"Well, now you have your answer, Mark. You made a difference," Ian said. "Not only in this life, but in the next. You were still here on earth so you could help bring Jody home too. It seems that you were the only one she would trust to take her."

"But, I can't leave now," he said. "Who will help you?"

"We'll figure things out here," Mary said. "You need to take Jody's hand and walk to the light."

Ian turned off his phone and smiled down at the child. "And I promise you, the music up there will be sweeter than any you've ever heard," he said.

Jody smiled up at him and patted her ear.

"Aye," Ian said, patting his own ear. "Just so."

Dr. Buus stooped down and scooped Jody up in his arms. Trustingly, she wrapped her arms tightly around his neck, and he straightened and turned to Mary and Ian. "Thank you," he said. "Thank you for finding us."

Then he walked forward to the corner of the room and disappeared from view.

"So, that's how it's done," Adeline said, dabbing at the tears in her eyes. "It's quite beautiful."

Mary nodded. "It's the best part of my job," she said. Then with a deep breath she turned to Ian. "And now, what are we going to do without Dr. Buus?"

Chapter Forty-six

The trio exited Jody's room and continued down the hall. "Tony's room is the next one," Ian said. "But I don't know who stayed there after he died."

"The asylum actually stopped using it beyond the first few years after Tony's death," Adeline said. "Unfortunately, it seemed that anyone placed in this room ended up committing suicide too."

"With Tony's help?" Mary asked.

"That would be my assumption," Adeline replied. "He was a predator after all."

Ian walked in the room first and looked around. It was nearly identical to Jody's room.

Adeline followed him in. "Just as I hoped," Mary heard Adeline say.

"What did you hope?" Mary asked as she entered the small room too.

"A mirror," Adeline replied. "This room has a mirror."

Mary looked at the mirror bolted to the wall and then looked back at Adeline. "You're right," she said. "Jody's room didn't have a mirror."

"It was part of his treatment," Ian said. "He was supposed to talk to himself and discuss his feelings."

"Was that his idea?" Adeline asked.

Ian thought about it for a moment and then nodded. "Aye, you've the right of it," he said. "He suggested it to Mark. He thought it would be helpful if he could see himself."

"Why? What's the big deal about Tony having a mirror in his room?" Mary asked.

"Mirrors, from ancient times, have been considered portals," Adeline said. "Especially paranormal portals."

Mary shook her head. "I've never heard of that," she replied.

"In your high school, they didn't talk about standing in front of a mirror and calling for Bloody Mary three times?" she asked.

"Well, yes, they did," Mary admitted.

"And didn't you ever hear of the superstition about seven years of bad luck if you broke a mirror? Adeline asked.

"Of course, but I never thought…" Mary stared.

"And did you ever hear about the custom of covering all the mirrors in a house in mourning so the spirit didn't accidentally get trapped in one?"

"That's why they covered mirrors?" Mary asked.

Adeline nodded. "Since the early Mesoamerican culture, mirrors have been considered portals to other realms. Even scrying bowls have reflective, mirror-like qualities."

"So, you think this mirror has served as some kind of a portal for Tony?" Ian asked.

Adeline nodded. "If he was as smart as we think, and had studied enough about the paranormal, he would have figured this out."

"And he asked for a mirror," Mary said.

"That mirror was always a creepy thing," a voice called out from the hallway.

Ian and Mary poked their heads out of Tony's room while Adeline slipped through the wall to see who had spoken. The ghost of a man in his mid-thirties stood in the doorway of the next room.

"Hello," Mary said. "I'm Mary, and you are?"

"Frank Marnette," he said with an easy smile. "I've been waiting a long time for you to come."

"You've been waiting for Mary?" Ian asked, stepping between Mary and the ghost.

"Naw, don't know nothing 'bout her personally," Frank replied. "I've been waiting for someone, anyone, to release us from this place."

"Why can't you leave?" Mary asked.

"Tony," Frank said. "Tony's spirit kind of rules this building, and we're all kind of stuck here until Tony goes away."

"He's not here now," Mary said.

"Don't matter," Frank said. "His hiding place is still here. It's got power."

"How does he get to his hiding place, Frank?" Adeline asked.

"That there mirror," Frank said. "I seen him hopping in and out of it myself. Once afore I died, but after that, plenty of times. 'Specially when they had other folks staying in that room."

Mary turned to Adeline and shook her head. "I will never, ever doubt the wisdom of a librarian," she said.

Adeline curtsied and smiled. "And now, I think we should find some tools and remove that mirror."

"Then what?" Mary asked.

"I believe," Ian said, "if we have his portal, we're in control."

"If you cover it, he can't get in," Adeline said. "If you destroy it, he doesn't have a place to hide."

"Hide from who?" Mary asked.

"Most of the spirits you've helped have simply had unfinished business here," Adeline said. "But they wanted to eventually go to the light, didn't they?"

Mary nodded. "Yes, they sometimes have tried to avoid it because they didn't want to leave someone they loved. But, they eventually wanted to find peace."

Nodding, Adeline smiled at Mary. "Yes, perfect choice of words, peace, eternal rest," she said. "But that was because they were good people, not perfect, but good. Tony studied religion. He had no doubt what was waiting for him at the end of life, unless he could hide from it. Instead of a light, Tony would have encountered the reward he deserved. Darkness."

"Darkness?" Mary repeated. "What kind of darkness?"

Adeline shook her head. "I don't know for sure," she said. "Some religions speak of fire and brimstone, some speak of avenging angels, some speak of vast darkness. I only believe it is something

Tony does not want to happen to him, which is why he is trying to enlarge his territory."

"To include Freeport," Mary said.

"At the very least," Adeline said.

Chapter Forty-seven

Even with the tools Ian had stored in the back of his SUV, it took them about twenty minutes to remove the mirror from the wall. Once it was removed, Ian took off his coat and placed it over the front of the mirror. Suddenly, spirits appeared all around them, gliding through the hallways and calling from the rooms.

Slowly, with Ian carrying the mirror in his arms, they made their way down the hall towards the entrance.

"Stop," one female ghost demanded, stopping in front of them. "What are you doing?"

Mary stepped up in front of Ian and spoke to the ghost. "We're leaving with the mirror," she replied. "We think it will help us stop Tony. Is this affecting you? Is there a problem?"

The woman looked confused and then slowly shook her head. "I don't understand why I've been here for so long," she said. "And I'm not sure what I should do next."

"Can you see a light?" Ian asked.

The woman didn't even look. "I've seen it," she said. "But it's too far away. I could never reach it."

"Well, try now," Ian encouraged her. "I think you might have the energy to do it now."

Still skeptical, the woman shrugged and begrudgingly looked around. Her eyes widened in wonder. "I see it," she breathed. "And it's close. I can touch…"

Suddenly, she was no longer in front of them.

Many of the other spirits, who'd watched the woman, began to search around too. And just as suddenly, one by one, the spirits started to disappear.

"How odd," Adeline said. "Could Tony's presence have trapped them here?"

Ian studied the scene for a few moments and then slowly nodded his head. "We know that paranormal beings exude energy," he said, reasoning as he spoke, "because that's how we measure their presence. If somehow Tony could absorb their energy so they were not strong enough to pass over, it would be, in a way, trapping them here."

Ian hefted the heavy mirror in his arms, repositioned it and started to walk up the hallway towards the lobby again.

"Then why would he want to leave?" Mary asked. "Why not stay here, absorbing their energy, maintaining his power over them?"

Ian froze and turned to Mary. "Because the power here was at status quo," he said, alarm in his voice. "And Tony wants more power."

He turned to Mary. "We need to get back home quickly," he said.

"Why?" she asked. "What did you just figure out?"

"You're a ghost magnet, Mary," he said. "You bring ghosts, and their energy, to you."

Mary glanced around the halls, watching as dozens of spirits floated past them and then disappeared. "But nothing like this," she said, shaking her head. "I get a couple of ghosts at a time. I don't have hundreds surrounding me."

Ian met her eyes, his bleak. "But what if you did, Mary?" he asked. "What if there were a huge calamity in Freeport? Where would all the spirits go?"

Mary's heart dropped, and she felt physically ill for a moment. "You can't think that Tony would be planning something..." she shook her head. "My house is not as big as the asylum. It couldn't hold..."

"The hospital," Ian said. "In just a few weeks you will be inside a hospital, along with several hundred other people."

"But I'd never let him do that," she argued. "I'd never let him keep them there."

Ian shook his head. "He'd only need you around until he trapped all the spirits in the building," he said. "You're only the bait. And the bait, once the trap is sprung, is expendable."

Mary shivered and nodded. "Okay, let's go home and figure out how we can stop him. At least we know we have several weeks."

Chapter Forty-eight

They carried the mirror to the SUV. Mary opened the tailgate and cleared a spot for the mirror to lay. Ian carefully laid it down, then reached into his tool box and pulled out a large roll of duct tape.

"Duct tape?" Mary asked. "Why do you need that?"

Pulling a long length from the roll, Ian ripped it off and taped one side of his coat to the other, securing the coat tightly around the mirror. "Well," he said, ripping off another length, "if he does derive some of his power from this mirror, I want to be very sure that as we are driving he isn't able to access any power."

Mary nodded. "Oh, really good point," she said, pulling another length from the tape and helping secure the mirror.

Once the coat was taped tightly around the mirror, they got into the SUV and headed back to Adeline's house.

"Do you mind if I take your files?" Ian asked the ghost.

She shook her head. "No, I don't mind at all," she said, meeting his eyes through the rearview mirror. "It will give you a reason to return, and I believe we have some things to discuss."

Ian nodded. "Aye, I believe we do," he agreed.

Confused and more than a little curious, Mary wanted to ask them what their covert conversation meant. She glanced over at Ian and saw that his eyes were now firmly fixed on the road ahead of him. Something was bothering him. Something had been bothering him since yesterday, but, she decided, if Ian wanted her to know, he'd tell her.

They pulled into the driveway at Adeline's home, left the mirror in the backseat, and quickly went in to pack their belongings.

Luckily, Mary thought as she scooped up her toiletries and placed them in her bag, she really hadn't unpacked, only taken out what she needed. She was packed up and eager to go in a few minutes. She rolled her suitcase into the hallway and stopped in her tracks when she saw Ian and Adeline quietly speaking together in the living room.

Ian was shaking his head sadly, but Adeline put her hand on his arm and spoke again. Ian quickly looked up at Adeline, hope in his eyes, and then turned away. Suddenly a highly ornate curio cabinet in the corner of the room opened and a sterling silver hand mirror floated across the room. Adeline put her hand out, and it landed gently in her palm.

Even from across the room, the beauty of the mirror took Mary's breath away. Although darkened with age, the carvings on the handle and edging of the mirror could still be clearly seen, and the luster of the silver still shone. Ferns, flowers and fairies embellished the mirror, melding within the flowing and intricate scroll work that was clearly created by a master's hand.

Adeline handed the mirror to Ian, and at first, he refused it. But she pressed it on him, and finally Mary heard her say, "*Credendo vides.*"

With a reluctant sigh and then a grateful nod, Ian accepted the mirror, bent down and placed it safely inside his suitcase. When he straightened, he saw Mary there and seemed a little uncomfortable.

"Sorry I took so long," Mary said, pretending she'd just joined them.

"Oh, no, no problem," Ian replied with a forced smile. "I was just saying goodbye to Adeline."

Mary came across the room to where they both stood. "Thank you for your hospitality," Mary said. "And your help. It was invaluable."

Adeline bent forward and kissed Mary on her cheek. Mary could feel the wisp of cold against her skin.

"Thank you for allowing me to help," the ghost replied. "I can't tell you how good it feels to be useful again. And I hope you will visit again."

Mary nodded. "I would really love to," she replied truthfully. "Your home is..." She paused to think of the right words.

Adeline smiled. "Otherworldly, perhaps?"

"Exactly," Mary replied. "It's like stepping away from the world for a little while."

"Well, anytime you need to step away from the world," Adeline invited, "you must come and see me."

Ian picked up his suitcase and nodded. "Thank you," he said.

"Don't hesitate to come back," Adeline urged, her eyes fixed on Ian. "Remember *credendo vides*."

"Aye, I'll remember," he said.

A few minutes later, their luggage was packed and Mary and Ian were both seated in the SUV. Ian reached over to place the car in reverse, but Mary placed her hand over his to stop him. He looked over at her, a question in his eyes.

"Just one question before we go," Mary said. "What does *credendo vides* mean?"

Ian sighed. "In believing, one sees," he said, and then he placed the car in reverse and backed out of the driveway.

Chapter Forty-nine

Mary hurried up the steps of the front porch to open the door for Ian who was carrying the large mirror in his arms, but before she could put her key in the lock, the door swung open.

"It's so great to have you home, sweetheart," Bradley said, stepping forward to take her in his arms. "I missed you."

She slipped to the side and smiled. "Just a moment, Bradley," she said. "We've got to get this inside."

Bradley stepped back when he saw Ian and the mirror and quickly moved any objects that might be a tripping hazard. Ian carried it across the room and carefully laid it on the couch.

He turned and grinned at Bradley. "And it's great to be home, darling," he replied. "I missed you too."

"What is that thing, and why is it wearing your coat?" Bradley asked.

"We should have a meeting," Mary said. "But first…"

"You have to go to the bathroom," Bradley and Ian said together.

Mary grinned. "Such a cute duet," she teased, and then she went upstairs to her bedroom.

They both waited to speak until the door closed. "So?" Bradley asked. "How is she doing?"

Ian smiled at him and nodded. "She's good," he said. "Actually, she's brilliant. You should have seen her handle the cop…"

He stopped, bit his lip and shook his head. "I probably shouldn't have mentioned that," he added.

Bradley folded his arms across this chest. "Yeah, probably not," he said, glancing up the stairs with a concerned look.

"It wasn't as bad as all that," Ian said. "Compared to the break-in…"

He stopped again. "I'm just going to sit down now and shut my mouth."

Ian walked over to the table, and Bradley followed him to the kitchen. "Did you guys stop and get lunch?" Bradley asked.

"No, we didn't want to risk it," Ian said, and when Bradley turned and stared at him, he shrugged. "Aye, I'll explain that comment when Mary gets down."

Mike appeared in the kitchen and looked around. "What did you bring into this house?" he asked, nearly frantic.

"A mirror from the asylum," Ian said. "And we think it was Tony's portal."

"It reeks of evil," Mike said.

"I'm sure it does," Ian said. "But before we destroy it, we need to have a plan."

Mary walked down the stairs and crossed into the kitchen. She sat down across from Ian. "Why do we need a plan?" she asked. "If we destroy it, he's caught."

Bradley sat down next to her and took her hand in his. "Okay, can we just start from the beginning here?" he asked. "So some of us can get up to speed."

Mary and Ian explained about the mirror being Tony's portal and described Adeline's theory about it being a hiding place.

"So if we destroy it, what happens?" Bradley asked.

"There's too much we don't know to answer that question," Mike said.

"Like what?" Mary asked.

"Like, is this his only portal, or could he use others?" Mike replied. "If we destroy it with him inside, is he trapped, or does he have another escape route? If we destroy it with him on the outside, can we control him or capture him?"

"I know that when we removed the portal from the asylum wall and covered it, all the spirits he was repressing were able to find the light," Ian said.

"So once you covered up his source of power, it became useless," Mike said. "But by bringing it here, have you increased his power here?"

Ian sat back in his chair and shook his head. "I hadn't even considered that," he said, distraught. "Have I made it worse?"

He pushed his chair away from the table and strode across the room. "Dammit! I should have seen the danger. I should have known…"

Mike glided over to him. "Hey. No. Stop," he said. "We don't know if what you did was the right thing or not. This is just conjecture on my part. Bringing it here would have probably been my decision too."

Ian took a deep breath and nodded. "Sorry for the dramatics," he said with a small smile. "We need cool heads to figure this out, not emotional ones."

"I have a question for the group," Bradley said. "How do you catch and contain a ghost?"

Chapter Fifty

"I ain't heard nothing so ridiculous in my life," Stanley exclaimed as the group sat around the table sharing a pizza. "Iffen they can go through walls, how do you think you can catch 'em?"

"Shhhh, Stanley," Rosie cautioned. "Clarissa is upstairs sleeping."

"Actually, she's at the Brennan's tonight," Mary said. "We just didn't feel good about her being in the same house as the mirror."

"Stanley has a point," Bradley said, getting back to Stanley's comment. "How do you contain something that has no substance?"

"How do you contain electricity?" Ian asked, selecting another piece of pizza and putting it on his plate. "It's just energy, like a ghost, but you can contain it and direct it."

"So we get ourselves a breaker box and flip a switch?" Stanley asked.

Ian smiled at Stanley. "Well, in a way, you're on the right track," he said. "There have been some experiments with a device called a Devil's Toy Box."

Rosie dropped her fork on her plate and shook her head. "Oh, Ian, I don't like the sound of that at all," she said. "We shouldn't be experimenting with the occult."

Ian placed his hand over Rosie's and gave it a comforting squeeze. "No, darling, it's not like that at all," he said. "It's just a name, like Devil's Food cake."

She sighed and smiled at him. "Oh, then that's okay," she said, picking up her fork. "And you say it's made of chocolate?"

"He didn't say that," Stanley inserted. "He just said that names don't make no mind. It's what the thing is what's important."

Rosie nodded. "Well, of course names don't matter," she said. "Unless, of course, it's named that because it does matter."

Ian met Mary's eyes across the table and grinned. Mary was relieved to see that this smile made it all the way to his eyes.

"Precisely," Ian said to Rosie, biting back a smile. "Now, this box is created by taking six mirrors, all the same size, and basically creating a six-sided cube with all the mirrors facing each other."

"Like an eternity box," Stanley said. "The reflections would keep on going back and forth."

"And back and forth," Rosie added.

"Exactly," Ian said. "The theory is that the infinite reflections confuse and trap the ghost because it doesn't know how to get out. Everywhere it turns, it's faced with its own reflection."

"How well has this worked?" Bradley asked.

Ian sighed. "And there's the rub," he said. "It's really hard to prove you have an entity trapped because you can't see inside."

"And if you open the box to measure the electro-magnetic power, it will exit the box," Mary added.

"Yes, that's right," Ian agreed. "So all we have now is theory."

Bradley shook his head. "This is a pretty dangerous situation to be testing a theory," he said. "Is there anything else out there?"

"There are some theories about using a Faraday cage," Ian said.

"Wait, I thought you said that was for protecting items from electro-magnetic influences," Bradley said.

"Well, yes, it is in most cases," Ian replied. "But in this case, you use the reverse. You lure the spirit into the trap and electrify the outside, effectively trapping them inside."

"And how do you know when they're inside?" Mary asked.

"You can use electromagnetic sensors to test for activity," Ian explained. "Then once you get action, you flip the switch."

"As long as your switch flipping is faster than the ghost," Stanley said.

Ian nodded. "Exactly."

Mary leaned back in her chair and glanced over at the coat-covered mirror on the couch. There was something wrong. She quickly got out of her chair and hurried over to the couch just in time to watch one of the lengths of duct tape yank itself free from the coat.

"Oh, no you don't," Mary cried, sitting on the couch and wrapping her arms around the coat and mirror.

A black shadow appeared on the wall behind the couch and slowly grew larger.

"Oh my goodness," Rosie squeaked. "It's coming after Mary."

Bradley jumped from his chair and ran across the room. "Get out of here!" he yelled.

But the shadow only grew.

Mary felt his presence growing in the room too. The malevolence was almost suffocating. She had to do something quickly, or Tony's evil would overpower her. "Ian," she called loudly. "Hand me the hammer. I'm going to destroy the mirror."

The shadow shook visibly and diminished slightly in size.

"Actually, I think a brick would be better," she said, and Tony shrunk some more.

She looked directly into the face of the shadow. "Get out of my house, or I will totally destroy your mirror," she said. "Get out now!"

The shadow lingered a moment longer until Ian approached with a hammer.

"You will not win!" he screamed, his voice echoing through the room. "You will not win!"

"Wanna bet?" Mary called as the shadow faded away.

She laid her head against Ian's coat and took a deep breath. "Well, that went well I think," she exclaimed softly.

"Iffen I wasn't standing right here watching it with my own eyes, I would have never believed it," Stanley said, still staring at the wall. "This is the shadow creature what's been spooking us all?"

Mary nodded. "Yes, that's him," she said. "And I think we were lucky."

"Well, we know the mirror's important to him," Ian said. "So at the very least we have bait."

"We have bait," Bradley said. "But are we sure we can catch and hold it?"

Chapter Fifty-one

Stanley and Rosie arrived home close to ten o'clock, both shaken and exhausted from their day.

"Stanley, that was the most frightening thing I've ever seen," Rosie said as they opened the door and turned on the light in the living room. "If this is what Mary does all the time, I don't know how she does it."

"I'm thinking this one is different," Stanley said. "It don't want her help. It wants something from her."

"But what?" Rosie asked. "What could it possibly want from Mary?"

He shook his head. "Can't say fer certain," he admitted. "But I can guarantee it ain't no good."

"Will you come and sleep in the bedroom tonight, Stanley?" Rosie asked. "I hate to admit it, but I'm frightened."

He kissed her tenderly and nodded. "Sure," he said. "Sure, I can sleep in there aside you. Why don't you go wash up? I got a couple o' things I told Ian I'd look up on the computer. Then I'll join you."

"Thank you, Stanley," she replied and walked towards their bedroom.

Stanley sat down on the chair in front of his computer and turned it on. He tapped his fingers impatiently, waiting for it to boot up. Then he typed in his password and waited for the main screen to appear.

"Are you done yet?" Rosie called out.

"No, not yet," he called back. "You go ahead and lay down. I won't be much longer."

He heard her shuffling around in the bedroom and then heard the sound of the springs from the bed. Good! She was laying down. Knowing his Rosie, soon as her head hit the pillow she would be fast asleep.

He opened up a browser window and typed in the search command "how do you catch a ghost." The first link he saw looked like an internet encyclopedia. "Well, this ought to be a good one," he mused softly. "Can't just anyone call themselves an encyclopedia."

The directions went through where to find ghosts, how to detect if you had a ghost, and finally, how to catch one. Then with fully animated instructions, they explained the candle method of catching a ghost.

"Take a large glass jar," Stanley read aloud softly. "Rosie's got them canning jars. Those ought to do the trick." He continued reading. "Put a candle in the bottom of the jar. Light the candle. The energy from the light will attract the ghost and he will enter the jar. Once you are sure the ghost is in the jar, place the lid over the jar and seal tightly."

Stanley smiled and nodded. "We don't need no goldurn Faraday cage," he said with a scoff of pride. "All we need is a jar and a candle. I'll show them what an old guy can do."

He stood up and walked down the hallway to check on Rosie.

The shadow flitted from behind the Christmas tree to the chair that Stanley had just occupied and studied the computer screen. The entity grew larger for a moment and then slipped back to the corner behind the tree.

Stanley peeked in to the bedroom. Sure enough, Rosie was sound asleep. He carefully pulled the door closed, being sure not to make a sound. He paused for a moment as a chill ran down his spine. Then shook his head. It was just his imagination, but just in case, he'd better make that trap and make it quickly.

The canning jars were on the top shelf of the cupboard. Stanley stared at them for a moment and then chose a quart jar, just to make sure there was enough room for that large ghost. He pulled a tea candle out of the drawer and set it inside the jar.

Looking around the room, he decided the best place for the trap was the coffee table. It was close to the Christmas tree but also pretty centered in the room. He moved the magazines and the Christmas bouquet onto the couch so the table was empty. Then he placed the jar on a ceramic coaster in the middle of the table.

He stepped back and nodded satisfactorily. The trap was set. Now all he had to do was get a lid, light the candle and wait.

Chapter Fifty-two

Stanley grabbed a plastic lid that would fit the jar and then stopped by the fireplace to remove the lighter wand from the mantle. Placing the lid in his pants pocket, he clicked the lighter on and then lowered it into the jar to light the candle.

A moment later, the candle flame was dancing in the bottom of the jar, casting shadows around the room. His heart beating rapidly, Stanley pulled the lid out of his pocket and kept his eyes glued on the jar, waiting for any signs of a shadow to appear inside the jar.

His arm up over his shoulder ready to pounce at a moment's notice, and his gaze focused on the coffee table, Stanley didn't notice the furtive shadow moving out from behind the tree.

"Come on, Tony," Stanley whispered. "I thought you liked flames. Come on, check out this flame."

Sniffing the air, Stanley was surprised to discover that the tiny tea candle was putting off such a strong odor. He hoped it wouldn't reach all the way to their bedroom, because then he'd have some explaining to do. Then he thought about Rosie's reaction when she learned that he'd caught the ghost all by himself. He didn't need Bradley. He didn't need Mary. And most of all, he didn't need that Casanova, Ian. He smiled and nodded.

Yeah, who would be Rosie's hero then?

The scent grew stronger, and then, in the corner of his eyes, Stanley saw flames. He spun around, terrified. The Christmas tree was ablaze, and the fire had already spread to the drapes and wall.

"Rosie!" he screamed. "Rosie, get out of the house!"

He started to run towards her when Tony appeared before him. Not a shadow, just a boy.

"Get out of my way," Stanley yelled at him.

Tony shook his head. "But I thought you liked flames, Stanley," the boy mocked. "And won't they all shake their heads when they blame the fire on you? Stupid, old man lighting candles at night."

Stanley stepped forward, and a piece of wood from the ceiling came crashing down onto his shoulder. He screamed with pain but knocked the stud away, pushing to get to Rosie. A blazing section of drywall fell forward, landing on his chest, but he pushed through the pain.

"Rosie!" he screamed. "Rosie!"

"Stanley?"

He heard her voice.

"Rosie, get out!" he yelled. "Get out through the window!"

I'm not going to leave you," she cried back.

"Don't worry," he gasped, feeling a new pain shooting down his left arm. "I can get out through the front door. Go now!"

He heard the bedroom window open, and he turned to Tony, who stood there looking down at Stanley with a smile on his face. "You didn't win," Stanley gasped. "You didn't win."

And then all went black.

Chapter Fifty-three

Mary sat in the recliner, her feet drawn up next to her, watching the fire crackle in the fireplace. Ian sat on one side of the couch and Bradley on the other, the mirror between them.

"It's interesting, isn't it," she mused, "that something so warm and comforting as a fire can also be terrifying."

"It's just a tool," Ian said. "The hands that yield it will determine the good or evil it does."

Mike appeared in the room and glided over to the coffee table. "Clarissa is sound asleep dreaming about Christmas," he said.

Mary sat up. "Do you realize that Christmas is less than a week away?" she exclaimed. "I don't have nearly enough gifts yet."

Bradley smiled at her. "I think we'll be fine," he said. "You have our entire closet filled with gifts as well as two shelves in the basement."

Mike turned and smiled at Mary. "What did you get me?" he asked.

"Aftershave," she teased.

"Funny," he replied. "Really funny."

She sat back in the chair and chuckled. "You're going to have to wait, just like everyone else," she said, and then she looked around the room. "I just realized how much my life has changed in one year."

Bradley nodded. "Yes, last year at this time we were working that job in Chicago," he said. "And I ended up at Cook County hospital."

"Remember that sweet, old man who died just as we were escaping?" she asked.

"You escaped from the hospital?" Ian asked. "Well, remember how you did it. It might come in handy."

"What do you mean?" Bradley asked.

"We were trying to figure out why Tony would leave the asylum," Ian explained. "Because he really was running the roost there. He was sucking energy from all the spirits in the place. He had a good deal. Why leave?"

"Power," Mike said.

"Yes, exactly," Mary agreed. "But then how could he get power from coming here? I don't see as many ghosts in a month to equal the number of spirits in the asylum."

"What did you come up with?" Bradley asked.

"That some event would have to occur in a large building, with Mary in it, in order to attract and trap the spirits for Tony," Ian said. "The only building with enough occupants would be the hospital."

"So, is he planning on waiting until the baby comes?" Bradley asked.

"No, he's not," Mike inserted.

"What do you mean?" Mary asked.

"You're assuming that the baby is the reason you'd be in the hospital," Mike explained. "But you'd be there if one of your family had been hurt, wouldn't you?"

"The fires," Mary said, nodding. "If he set fire to our house…"

"Well, he's not going to burn this house down," Ian said. "Not with his mirror in it. And, except for making sure he doesn't try and open it, we're fairly safe."

Mary sighed. "It feels good to not worry," she laughed. "Goldurn good."

Then she sat up and her eyes widened. "Stanley and Rosie," she said, a pit growing in her belly. She turned to Mike. "Mike…"

"On my way," he said and then disappeared.

He reappeared a moment later. "You've got to get over there," he said. "Their house is on fire."

Chapter Fifty-four

The cruiser flew down the side streets to Rosie and Stanley's house. They could see flames in the window when they turned onto the street. Bradley pulled the cruiser over the sidewalk and across their front lawn, stopping just in front of the porch.

Rosie was on the porch in her nightgown, pounding on the front door. She turned, tears rushing down her face, when she saw them.

"He's inside!" she screamed. "He's trapped inside."

"Where?" Bradley asked, knowing they would probably not be able to see because of the smoke.

"The living room," she said. "He told me to climb through the bedroom window. He promised he'd come through the front door. The key won't fit. The lock's melted."

"Go sit in the cruiser, Rosie," Bradley said. "And wait for the fire department, okay?"

She nodded and hurried down the steps.

Bradley turned to Ian. "Ready?" he asked.

Ian nodded. The two men took a couple of steps backward and then rushed at the door, ramming their shoulders and arms against it. The door gave slightly, but wasn't quite open.

"Again," Ian said.

They stepped back and rushed it again, the door splintering in the center and breaking open. Flames, invigorated by the fresh air, blazed before them, and smoke as black as pitch enveloped them.

"Stanley!" Bradley called. "Stanley, where are you?"

Down on all fours, Bradley moved towards the kitchen, and Ian moved towards the hall.

A piece of burnt drywall lay at an angle on the floor. Ian kicked it to the side and gasped. Stanley lay motionless underneath the rubble.

"Bradley, over here!" Ian yelled.

Stanley body was burnt, his shirt melted to his flesh, and his eyes were closed.

Ian leaned over and pressed his hand to Stanley's neck, searching for a pulse.

Chapter Fifty-five

Mary sat on the couch, a hammer in her hand, guarding the mirror. But her focus was on her cell phone next to her. Bradley, Ian and Mike had been gone for more than an hour, and she hadn't heard anything about the fire. She picked up the phone, tempted to dial Bradley's number, but she realized he was dealing with a crisis and would call when he could.

No sooner had she placed the phone down than Mike appeared next to her. His face was drawn, and he looked worse than she'd ever seen him.

"What?" she asked, tears pooling in her eyes. "What happened? How are they?"

"Rosie's fine," Mike said. "She had a little smoke inhalation and minor burns. They're taking her to the hospital for overnight evaluation."

"Stanley?" she asked, her throat tightening.

Mike shook his head. "Not so good," he said.

"He's not…" she began.

"No," Mike said, coming closer and sitting on the coffee table in front of her. "No, he's not dead. But it looks like the fire started in the living room where Stanley was located. He was burned, and he inhaled a lot of smoke. He…"

Mike sighed and met her eyes, his own now filled with tears. "He won't wake up," he said. "He's in a coma. They don't know if…"

Mary stood up, wiped her eyes with her sleeves and hurried over to the closet. "I have to go to them," she said. "I have to see Rosie. I have to see Stanley. Mike…"

She leaned against the wall and started to sob. "It's my fault, Mike," she cried, her voice catching. "It's all my fault. If he dies… If he dies…"

Mike moved to stand in front of her. He put his hands on her shoulders, and she could feel the cold pressure. Tears streaming down her face, she lifted her eyes to look at him.

"If he dies he gets to go back home," Mike said. "Isn't that what you told me?"

She shook her head. "I don't care what I said. I don't want him to die."

She reached into the closet and pulled out her coat.

"You can't go," Mike said.

"He might be dying," she replied. "I might never see him again. I have to at least say goodbye."

"You can't go," Mike said.

"I don't care," she cried. "I don't care about the mirror. I don't care about any damn spirit. I don't care about anything except seeing Rosie and Stanley."

She had her hand on the door and was about to open it when Mike said, "and what happens if Tony detonates the hospital once you walk in that door because now he has you where he wants you?"

Her hand dropped from the doorknob, and she leaned her head against the door, her body shaking as she cried. "This isn't fair, Mike," she cried, her voice thick with tears. "This wasn't supposed to happen to them."

Mike came up behind her and whispered. "I know, Mary. This is so unfair. This is so hard," he said. "Does it help you to know that God is crying too?"

She shook her head. "No. No it doesn't," she said. Then she paused. "Okay. A little. It helps a little."

She pulled a tissue out of her coat pocket and wiped her nose, then turned to look at Mike. "It hurts, Mike," she whispered. "It hurts all the way to my soul."

He nodded. "I know, sweetheart," he said. "But Stanley would want you to be strong for him."

She took a shuddering breath and nodded. "No," she said. "He'd want me to be goldurn angry."

Mike smiled. "And are you?"

She shook her head, and more tears flowed down her cheeks. "No," she whispered through her tears. Then she took a gulping breath. "No. Because I'm too scared for him."

Chapter Fifty-six

Bradley stood next to the window looking into the burn unit surgical suite as the doctors cleaned and debrided Stanley's burnt arms and torso. It was almost a blessing that Stanley was unconscious, Bradley thought, so he didn't feel the surgeons removing the damaged skin and irrigating the area with a saline solution to prepare it for an eventual skin graft.

An array of IVs surrounded the top of the bed, and a heart monitor pulsed a steady, slow beat, assuring him that even though Stanley looked pale and wan, he was indeed still alive. The door behind him opened, and Ian, covered in the same black soot as Bradley, walked up beside him and looked at the procedure.

"How's he doing?" Ian asked.

Bradley shrugged and took a breath before he spoke. "He's still alive," he said, his voice breaking slightly. "How's Rosie?"

"She's fine," he said with a sad smile. "Well, she's fine physically. She's near frantic that they won't let her see Stanley. I told her I'd flash my doctor badge and see what I could find out."

"I should have known he'd be after them," Bradley said quietly, but Ian could hear the restrained anger in his voice. "I should have forced them to spend the night."

Ian shook his head. "Why do we do that to ourselves?" he asked.

Bradley turned and looked at him. "What?"

"Why do we take the blame upon ourselves when a loved one is hurting?" he asked. "I do it myself. As a matter of fact, I was just blaming myself for not thinking of the whole hospital scenario earlier so we could have warned Stanley and Rosie. Why do we do it?"

"It wasn't your fault," Bradley said.

"Aye, and it wasn't yours either," Ian replied. "And really, if we want to go down that road, it wasn't Mary's fault that Tony was drawn to her because of her ability."

"It was God's fault," Bradley said. "If he hadn't given Mary that choice—"

"She'd be dead now," Ian interrupted.

Bradley sighed and laid his head against the glass window, the coldness relieving the heat on his face. "So whose fault is it?" he asked. "Because it has to be someone's fault."

Ian winced as he placed his hand on Bradley's shoulder. With no coat to protect him, the splinters from Stanley's door had pierced his shirt and embedded themselves in his skin. Eventually he'd need to remove them, but for now, he had more to worry about than just a few pieces of wood.

"Well, we can certainly blame Tony," he said. "Because whether or not he can feel remorse, he does know right from wrong. And he chose to do evil."

He sighed and looked at Stanley, looking even older than usual. "And I suppose if we really need to blame someone, we can place a little blame on Stanley for being a stubborn, old coot with too much pride," he said, his voice catching and his eyes misting over. "But I wouldn't change him for the world."

Bradley wiped his hands over his eyes and nodded. "I haven't called Mary," he admitted. "I don't think I'm strong enough to hear her tears."

"Aye, I understand," Ian said. "I'm sure Mike's told her by now."

"When we broke through the door and I saw Stanley on the ground, I thought…" Bradley shook his head and took a deep breath. "I thought he was dead."

Ian nodded. "So, did I," he said. "And I've never been so grateful to feel someone's pulse before in my life."

"He has to be fine," Bradley whispered harshly. "He has to pull through and be fine."

"If love counts," Ian said, "he'll pull through."

Each man, unbeknownst to each other, thought about their respective fathers at that exact moment, thought about how they were taken away from them much too early in their lives.

Bradley sighed. "Sometimes love doesn't count," he said sadly. "We think it should, but it doesn't always count."

"Aye, that's the truth," Ian agreed. "But this time. This time it has to count."

Chapter Fifty-seven

Bradley and Ian watched the surgery for a few more minutes, Ian's hand still on Bradley's shoulder. Then Ian carefully removed it and started to step away. Bradley turned and met Ian's eyes.

"Thank you," he said, and he gave Ian an appreciative pat on the arm. He was instantly alarmed when he saw the look of intense pain and the sudden paleness on Ian's face. "What the hell?" Bradley asked. "What's wrong?"

Ian tried to shrug it off. "I just got a few splinters in my arm when we broke down the door," he said. "I'm fine. You watch Stanley, and I'll—"

"The hell you will," Bradley said. He hurried over to the door and motioned for a nurse. "Can you get a doctor in here? Ian was injured during the fire, and I'd really like someone to look at it."

Bradley turned back and studied his friend. He noticed the rips and tears along the side of his shirt. "Why didn't you tell me?" he asked.

"It's not a big deal," Ian insisted. "I was going to get some tweezers out of my toiletry kit when I got back to your place."

There was a knock on the door, and a young, female doctor entered. "Chief Alden?" she asked. "Is there something you need?"

"Thank you, Dr. Abid," Bradley replied. "Ian had a run in with a door when we were breaking into the house. I was wondering if you could just look at him."

Ian shook his head. "Really, it's nothing," he said. "A few splinters…"

"Can you pull your shirt over your head?" Dr. Abid asked.

Ian reached up, then stopped, his face contorted in pain. "No, I don't suppose I can," he said.

"Sit down," she ordered with a tone that brooked no argument. Ian immediately obeyed.

She went to the door and spoke to a nurse for a moment. Almost immediately a stainless steel cart with medical supplied was wheeled into the room. Dr. Abid picked up the scissors and carefully cut through the arm of Ian's shirt. When she pulled the cloth away, Bradley gasped.

"Dammit Ian," he said.

Ian's arm was covered in an oozing coating of blood, the splinters acting as tiny stoppers so more blood hadn't escaped. Ian looked down and then turned to Bradley. "It wasn't a high priority," he said, and Bradley knew exactly what he meant.

"Well, it is now," Bradley replied. "What do you think, doctor?"

She shook her head slowly as she examined his arms. "First, I need to get permission from the patient to share this information with you," she said. She glanced up at Ian. "May I continue?"

He smiled and nodded. "Aye, go ahead."

She nodded at him, and then her gaze returned back to his arm. "The small ones can be removed with tweezers," she said. "But there are also larger ones that might have caused muscle or tendon damage. We'll have to do a CT scan to be sure."

"I really don't think this is that big of a deal," Ian said.

"Perhaps not to you," she said. "But the splinters are not the only problem. The possibility of infection is also a concern. I would like to start you on an IV of antibiotics immediately."

"Wait. I have things to do…" Ian began.

Ignoring his protests, the doctor picked up the scissors and cut the rest of his shirt off his body. His torso was riddled with painful looking bruises. "Did this happen today?" she asked.

Ian shook his head. "No, it's several weeks old," he answered. "I had a run in with someone who wasn't happy to see me."

"Did you see a medical professional about this?" she asked.

Ian smiled and nodded. "Aye, I did," he said.

The doctor straightened up. "There does not appear to be any new damage to your torso, but we need to extract the splinters as soon as possible." She studied him for a long moment. "I assume that you would prefer a topical anesthetic than an injection."

Ian nodded. "I think I've had far enough things poking through my skin today," he agreed. "Topical would be a lovely choice. Thank you."

The doctor left the room to order the scan and the medications.

Bradley shook his head. "You're a mess," he said with a gentle grin.

"Aye, I know," Ian replied. "And really, we don't have time for this."

"We'll make time," Bradley insisted. "I'll call Mary and let her know what's up. Then, while you have your scan, I'll check in with Rosie."

Ian sighed. "You won't be helping me break out of the hospital like Mary helped you?" he asked.

"No way, man," Bradley said. "You look like a backwards porcupine. Besides, all I had was a bullet wound."

Chapter Fifty-eight

The phone rang, and Mary reached for it immediately. "Bradley!" she cried. "Are you okay?"

"I'm fine," he immediately said, chiding himself for making her wait so long. "But I'm stuck here at the hospital for a while."

"That's fine. You do whatever you need to do," she said, leaning back on the couch. "How's Stanley?"

Bradley leaned back against the tiled wall of the hospital and ran his hand through his hair, surprised to find a few chunks of wood. "He went through surgery just fine," he said.

"Surgery?" Mary exclaimed.

"He had third-degree burns on his arms and his torso," Bradley replied. "They had to clean them in order to prepare them for skin grafts."

"And?" she asked.

"And his heart rate was solid throughout the operation, but he hasn't regained consciousness yet," Bradley said.

"What's the prognosis?" she asked.

"I'm heading down to see Rosie after our call, and I'll find out," he said. "I promised Ian I'd report back to her."

Mary sat up. "What's wrong with Ian?"

"He had a run in with a door," Bradley said. "His arm is riddled with splinters, some a pretty good sized, so they are going to run a scan to make sure there's no muscle or tendon damage and then remove them."

"Ouch," Mary said. "But other than that?"

"He's good," he said. "He's fine."

Mary sniffed back the tears, but her voice was filled emotion. "I really wish I could be there with you," she said, her voice shaking.

"Yeah, I wish you could be too," he replied. "But, we both know…"

She nodded. "Yes, I know," she said. "It's just what Tony wanted."

"And we are not going to give Tony what he wanted," Bradley said, his voice determined.

"No. No we're not," Mary agreed.

She was quiet for a long moment, and finally she said. "Bradley, I love you."

"I love you too, sweetheart," he replied. "I'm not sure when I'll be home, but if you need me, call."

She nodded, a lone tear trickling down her cheek. "I will," she said, "I promise."

Chapter Fifty-nine

Mary hung up the phone and placed it on the coffee table in front of her. Then she put her hands on her belly and looked down as her unborn child moved beneath her hands. She took a deep breath and nodded. "Okay, Mikey," she said with determination. "You and I are going to war."

"Mike," she called out. "Mike."

Immediately, Mike appeared in front of her. He studied her closely and noticed the fire in her eyes that had recently replaced the sorrow.

"No. Whatever it is you are thinking about, the answer is no," he said.

"I want you to stay at the Brennan's and watch over Clarissa," she said, ignoring his words.

"Mary, you can't take this thing on by yourself," he said.

Eyes blazing, she turned on him. "Do you know that?" she asked. "Do you one hundred percent know that I can't beat him? Or are you just saying that because you're worried about me?"

Mike shook his head. "Well, no, I don't know one hundred percent—"

"Did God tell you that I couldn't defeat Tony?" she interrupted. "Did He?"

"No," Mike said. "But remember, that first night…"

"I was afraid that first night," she admitted. "But I'm not afraid anymore. I'm mad. I'm really mad. Tony is not going to come floating into my life and mess with my friends and my family. He is going down."

"Mary, please…"

"Mike, do you trust me?" she asked, and then she shook her head. "No, even better, do you trust God? Because He obviously handed this one off to me."

Mike opened his mouth and then closed it, shaking his head. "I don't want anything to happen to you," he said softly.

She sighed and nodded. "Me neither," she said. "I have way too much to live for. But I won't let this spirit bully and hurt my family anymore. My choice, Mike. My freewill choice."

He nodded, knowing he was obligated to respect her decision. "I love you, kid," he said as he faded away.

"I love you too, Mike," she replied.

Once she knew he was gone, she walked across the room to the hall closet. She pulled out the Louisville Slugger baseball bat her brothers had given her for home protection. She hefted it up, took a couple of practice swings and smiled. Yeah, she could still knock it out of the ball park.

She walked back to the couch with the bat in her arms and bent to unstrap the mirror. Then she stopped, put the bat down and folded her arms to pray. "Dear God. First let me apologize for being angry with you this evening. I know that you gave us all freewill and choice, and sometimes people choose to harm others. I know it's not your fault. I was just sad and frightened and angry. I'm grateful for my friends and my family, and I pray that you will watch over them and bless them. Bless Stanley. Help him to heal." She paused and wiped the tears from her cheeks. "Please help me this night, Father. Help me to defeat Tony. Help me to be guided and know what to do. And mostly Father, help me to be brave. Amen."

Mary bent down, pulled the duct tape away from Ian's coat and unwrapped the mirror. It seemed to glow dully as it reflected the light in the room. She picked up the bat and swung. The area was too tight. She pushed the mirror out to the middle of the room and tried another practice swing.

Perfect.

She took a deep breath, positioned herself into a batter's stance and yelled, "Tony. I've got something you'll want to see."

Chapter Sixty

"Mary. Mary," Tony's voice echoed eerily around the living room.

Mary listened, but the fear didn't come. Confidence and raging fury were her main emotions now.

"Cut the crap, Tony," she said. "It's not working anymore."

He appeared across the room from her. "You should have seen Stanley," he said. "Burnt to a crisp and lying on the floor." He laughed, an evil, menacing sound. "I don't think he'll live for much longer. You'll probably want to go see him at the hospital."

"That's it," Mary said, and she swung the bat into the mirror.

CRACK.

The mirrored surface cracked in half.

"What are you doing?" Tony screamed.

Mary shrugged calmly. "Just warming up," she replied and swung again.

CRACK.

One half of the mirror broke into smaller pieces.

"You can't do that!" he screamed, coming closer. "I can kill you. I can kill you and your baby."

Mary turned to him. "No, you can't," she said. "You can't hurt me. You can't hurt my child. And you will no longer hurt my family and friends."

A small fire burst in the corner of the room. "Wanna bet?" he screamed.

"Yes," Mary said, whipping the bat against the surface of the mirror. "I do."

"Stop it!" he screamed, as the mirror scattered further.

"You can't hide anymore," Mary said. "You are going to face judgement for what you've done."

"No," he exclaimed. "I'm not."

Another small fire started next to the Christmas tree. "And you are going to burn," he threatened.

The fires licked at the carpet and the base of the tree. Mary could smell the acrid scent of smoke. She took a deep breath and held firm. "No, I'm not going to burn," she said, and she struck the mirror again. "You are."

"Who do you think you are?" he screamed.

She brought the bat up over her shoulder and then whipped it down with all of her might, sending pieces of glass up in the air. "I am Mary O'Reilly Alden, and I am done with you."

He stopped and looked down at the shattered mirror. Then he looked at Mary and started to laugh, the sound echoing throughout the house. "Oh, you think so?" he asked mildly.

He glanced over his shoulder and smiled. Another fire started in the kitchen. He glanced the other way, and another fire started near the front door. Mary looked around. Every way out of the room was now blocked by fire.

"You're not done with me," he said. "You're stuck with me. I will be with you forever, destroying everything and everyone you love."

"Like you destroyed your own family?" Mary asked.

He scoffed at her. "Oh, don't try the guilt thing Mary," he said. "They displeased me. They were annoying, and they had to die."

"And Jody? What about Jody?" she asked.

He shrugged. "I was bored," he said, shaking his head. "And really, she was not much entertainment."

He glanced at the couch, and a fire started in one of the cushions, the smell of burning cloth stinging Mary's eyes.

"You have been much more entertaining, Mary," he said. "It's too bad, actually, that you're going to have to die. But I'm sure your power is going to be delectable."

Mary shivered but didn't let herself waiver.

The smoke was making it hard for Mary to breathe. "If I die, you won't get what you wanted," she managed to say.

He shrugged. "That friend of yours, Ian," he said. "He will give me what I need." Then his smile widened. "Actually, he can give me more than I ever imagined."

"You are not going to win," she said, praying silently that a solution would present itself.

"Oh, Mary," he laughed. "I already have."

Chapter Sixty-one

Mary's eyes were burning and her lungs felt like they were going to explode as she gasped for air. The heat in the room was increasing and the thick smoke made it impossible to see anything, she had no way to escape.

Dear God, she prayed, I really don't want to die like this.

Suddenly, the smell of the smoke started to dissipate and a cold breeze whipped through the room. Suddenly she could breathe again. Like a lid over a pot, the smoke was tamped down and she could see around the room. The blazing fires slowed and died. Then, the damage started to reverse itself, as if there had never been a fire.

Tony glanced around the room. "What happened?" he asked. "What did you do?"

Mary hungrily took a deep breath of the fresh air. The scent of pine and vanilla filled the room, covering over any remaining smell of smoke. An instant image of her grandmother standing in the kitchen, letting Mary lick the beaters came to her mind. The vision was so clear, it was if she'd been transported back to one of her favorite Christmas memories. Suddenly, she realized who the second shadow was.

"I didn't do anything, Tony," she said, finally understanding. "But there entities far more powerful than you."

A shadowed figure stepped out from the kitchen, and finally, Mary's guess was confirmed.

"Hello Mary," the kindly spirit said, his voice low and deep. "I've been asked to help you with this matter." He turned to Tony. "Do you know who I am?"

Tony's eyes widened and he shook his head. "I don't believe in you," he exclaimed, although Mary could now hear the fear in Tony's voice. "You're nothing but a fairy tale."

The ancient spirit shook his head, his white beard brushing against the fur on his collar. "I'm afraid you are sadly mistaken," he said. "And I'm afraid that you have a lot to answer for."

"I'm stronger than you," Tony screamed as the spirit approached him. "I can control you."

The spirit laughed softly at the absurdity of Tony's words. "There is nothing stronger than the Spirit of Christmas," he said. "Especially during this time of year."

Laying a red gloved hand on Tony's shoulder, he sought Tony's eyes. "You will accompany me now," he said. "And you will not return to earth again."

Tony struggled against the hold, but could not move.

"Mary," the kindly spirit said. "You were very brave."

Then he and Tony disappeared.

Chapter Sixty-two

Mary made her way carefully through the broken shards of mirror, pulled on her coat and grabbed her purse and keys. She opened the door and was greeted by the first snowflakes of a new snow. She stopped on the porch and lifted her head, letting the delicate flakes land on her face. They were like tiny, celestial kisses, soothing her fire-warmed skin and melding with her hot tears to offer cooling relief.

She took a deep breath of the cold night air, let it fill her lungs and cleanse the last vestiges of Tony's smoke from her body. She looked out from her porch. Christmas lights from all of the homes around her twinkled in the night. The snow swirled around the light posts and the bare tree branches, dusting everything with a blanket of white. She felt an overwhelming sense of peace in her heart. She stayed for a moment longer, relishing the tranquility of the moment, then carefully climbed down the stairs and headed to her car.

The emergency room was empty when Mary approached the receptionist's desk. The orderly looked up from the computer and looked at Mary.

"Stay right there," he said. "I'll be right around with a wheelchair."

"But—" Mary began.

"No buts," the orderly said, hurrying from behind the plexiglass enclosure and wheeling a chair towards Mary. "Those are hospital rules. Now, is your husband coming?"

"He's already here," Mary said.

The orderly was taken aback. "He's already here?" he asked.

Mary nodded. "He's been here for hours," she tried to explain, sitting in the chair.

"Well, he should have brought you with him," he said. "What was he thinking?"

Suddenly, Mary realized what the confusion was all about. "Oh, wait, I'm not having a baby," she said.

The orderly backed up a step and looked at her in disbelief.

She shook her head. "No, I mean I'm not having a baby tonight," she corrected. "My husband, Chief Alden, is here with several of our friends. They were involved in a house fire tonight. I need to see how they're doing."

"Oh," he said with a smile. "Well, that makes sense. Sure, I'll let you in." He helped her out of the chair. "The one with the splinters is in room six. The other two have been taken upstairs. I believe Chief

Alden is with the woman, up in room three. The other one, the old man, he's up in isolation."

He pressed a button, and the doors to the emergency room area opened.

"Thank you," Mary said. Then she hurried down the hall.

Stopping at room six, she knocked on the door.

"You can come in," Ian called.

She entered the room. Ian was sitting on an examination table, bare chested, his arm covered with gauze. "Mary!" he exclaimed, hopping off the bed and hurrying over to her. "You can't be here. We don't know what Tony—"

"Tony's gone, Ian," she said. "We don't ever have to worry about him again."

"Gone?" Ian asked, amazed. "How did you… Are you okay?"

She nodded, surprised when she felt tears form in her eyes. She quickly brushed them away and nodded again. "It's been a pretty long day," she said, her voice breaking.

He took her in his arms and hugged her. "Aye, it has at that," he said.

Stepping back, his hands still on her upper arms, he met her eyes. "Have you seen Bradley yet?" he asked.

"No," she replied, shaking her head. "I just got here."

"Ah, well then, let's go search him out," he said, leading her towards the door.

"What about your shirt?" Mary asked.

Ian shrugged. "Well, the one I came with is in the trash bin, cut in pieces and no good for anything anymore," he explained. "And although I've had an army of nurses coming in and out of the room to check on me, none of them seem to be able to locate a shirt for me."

Mary couldn't stop the grin. "I just bet they couldn't," she said.

"What?" he asked.

"Ian, the only thing better than the black shirt," she teased, "is no shirt."

"Mary, you're just flattering me," he said. "I'm a fair mess, with my scrapes and bruises. No one in their right mind would find this body attractive."

She shook her head. "You just keep believing that."

Ian led her to the elevator, and they took it up to the third floor. "Rosie's room is down this hall," he said. "As far as I know, she hasn't been able to see Stanley yet, and she's frantic."

"I don't blame her," Mary replied. "I would be frantic too." She stopped just before Rosie's room and turned to Ian. "How is Stanley? Really?"

He shook his head. "He's not good," he answered softly. "The doctors believe he might have suffered a heart attack during the fire. Then, there was a lack of oxygen because of the smoke. And on top of that, third degree burns. It all depends on how much his body can take."

Mary nodded, wiped away the escaping tears and took a deep breath. "He's a fighter," she said. "If nothing else, Stanley's a fighter."

Ian nodded. "Aye, he is," he agreed quietly. "Aye, he is."

Chapter Sixty-three

"Oh, Mary," Rosie cried. "It was so frightening. Stanley was inside the burning house, and I couldn't get to him. I tried, but I just couldn't."

Mary looked down at Rosie's bandaged hands, burnt raw from her efforts to turn the searing doorknob, and wrapped her arms around her friend. "You did everything you could," Mary said. "Stanley will be so proud of you when he hears how hard you tried."

"I shouldn't have left him," Rosie cried into Mary's shoulder. "I should have gone into the hallway."

"Nonsense," Mary replied gently. "You did exactly what you were supposed to do. Exactly what Stanley wanted you to do."

"I was so frightened, Mary," Rosie admitted.

"Well, of course you were," Mary comforted. "Anyone would have been frightened in that situation. The fact that you got yourself out the window and around to the front of the house was amazing. And Ian told me that you gave them all the information they needed to get Stanley out. You saved his life, Rosie."

Rosie lifted her head and looked at Mary. "Really?" she asked, her voice shaking with hope.

Mary nodded. "Really," she said.

Rosie seemed to relax at Mary's words. "I had no idea," she said, trying to muffle a yawn.

"Why don't you try to sleep for a little while?" Mary suggested. "There's nothing that heals a body better than sleep."

Rosie nodded and settled back into the pillows. "That's a good idea," she said sleepily. "I'll just take a nap."

Mary leaned forward and kissed Rosie's cheek. "Sweet dreams," she whispered.

Lifting the control switch from the side of the bed, Mary turned down the lights, and then she quietly left the room.

Bradley and Ian were in the hall, waiting for her.

"She's going to sleep for a little while," Mary said.

"I don't know how you did it," Bradley said, shaking his head. "I've been trying to convince her to sleep for the last hour."

"Well, I'm sure having someone reinforce that she'd done everything she could had a lot to do with it," Mary said. "I didn't even have to mention to her that Tony was gone."

Bradley nodded. "And that's something we need to talk about," he said.

"Aye, I'm interested in hearing about how you did it too," Ian agreed. He looked up and down the hall. "But where can we go to speak?"

"There's a private viewing room attached to Stanley's isolation room," Bradley said. "We could go up there, check on his progress and then have a conversation about what happened." He looked over at Mary. "And I have a feeling I'm not going to be too thrilled with the story."

She sighed and nodded. "Yeah, I have the same feeling too."

Chapter Sixty-four

Mary, Bradley and Ian took the elevator up to the fourth floor in silence. The elevator doors opened in front of the nurse's station. One of the nurses looked up from her computer monitor and addressed Bradley.

She shook her head sadly. "There's been no change," she said.

"Thank you, "Bradley said. "We're just going to sit in the observation room."

"Okay," she replied. Then she looked at Ian. "Would you like something to wear? It gets cold in those observation rooms."

He smiled at her. "That would be much appreciated," he said.

She got up and walked to the back of the station, opened a large drawer and pulled out a sweatshirt with the hospital's logo emblazoned on it. "Here," she said, handing it to him. "That will keep you warm."

He pulled it over his head and carefully pushed his arm through the sleeve. It was a little loose on him, but it was warm and soft.

"Just don't tell anyone I gave it to you," she said with a warm smile.

"Why?" Ian said. "I don't want you to be in trouble for giving it to me. I'll gladly pay for it."

She shook her head. "No, that's not it," she replied. "I have some colleagues who would have preferred to keep you shirtless."

Mary smiled and held back a laugh. "Thank you," she said to the nurse. "Your secret is safe with us."

They walked down the hall, and Bradley opened the door to the observation area that corresponded to Stanley's room. Mary gasped softly and walked over to the window. The purple bruises on Stanley's face stood out boldly against the pale color of his skin. And oxygen mask covered his nose and his mouth, and a myriad of IV tubes and monitor wires traveled down alongside his body.

"Where did they put his IVs?" Mary whispered.

"In his leg," Bradley replied. "There was no place on his arms that wasn't burnt."

Stanley's head was wrapped with gauze, and his arms, chest and torso were covered with a special blanket for burns. The only sign of life was the monitor in the corner that slowly registered his heart beat.

She stared at Stanley, willing him to move, willing his eyes to open, but his condition didn't change. "When will they know if he had a heart attack?" she asked.

"They won't know until he wakes up and they do an EKG," Bradley said.

She put her hand on his arm. "He will wake up," she said with determination. "He's a fighter. He will wake up."

Bradley took a deep breath and nodded. Then he turned to her. "You would tell me, right?" he asked. "You would tell me if his spirit was no longer in his body."

She looked up at him. "Yes, of course, I would tell you," she said.

He nodded, not trusting himself to speak, and then turned back to the window.

After a few moments of silence, he turned back to her. "I don't want to know," he said.

"What?" she replied, confused.

"I don't want to know what you did to get rid of Tony," he said. "I'm grateful that he can't do this to anyone else we love."

She wrapped her arms around his arm and leaned against him. "Me too," she said, tears flowing freely. "Me too."

Chapter Sixty-five

"Is Grandpa Stanley coming home for Christmas?" Clarissa asked as the family sat in the living room on Christmas Eve.

"No, sweetheart," Rosie said sadly. "He still has to be in the hospital."

"But it's Christmas," Clarissa replied, shaking her head. "He shouldn't be alone on Christmas."

"He won't be alone, sweetheart," Mary said. "We're all going to take turns watching over him."

Clarissa smiled at Mary. "And when he wakes up, he's going to see the card I made him, right?" she asked.

"Yes, he is," Bradley said. "And if that doesn't cheer him up, I don't know what will."

Rosie wept softly and tried to pull a tissue from a box with her bandaged hands. Mary quickly reached over, pulled one out for her and placed it in between her fingers. Rosie blotted the tears from her eyes. "Thank you," she whispered.

"I miss Grandpa Stanley, too," Clarissa said, walking over to Rosie and giving her a hug.

Rosie smiled, her eyes moist with tears. "Yes, dear," she said. "We all miss Grandpa Stanley."

Ian came across the room, bent over and kissed Rosie on the top of her head. "I'll be leaving for my turn," he said. "And I'll tell him I'm making googly eyes at his wife. That'll wake him up for sure."

Rosie reached up and patted Ian's arm. "And then he'll call you a foreigner," she said with a sad laugh.

"Aye," Ian replied, his voice breaking. "And he'll tell me I have a funny accent."

He took a deep breath, dashed the tears away and stood.

"Are you sure you don't want to stay for Christmas?" Mary asked.

He came to her and gave her a hug. "No, darling, I need to be back in Chicago," he said. "So, I'll take my turn with Stanley and then I'll be on the road."

Bradley walked over and hugged Ian. "Merry Christmas."

Ian smiled. "Merry Christmas to you too."

Mike glided over to Ian. "If you need anything," he said, "anything at all, call me."

Ian nodded. "I'll just call out your name," he began.

Mike grinned. "And you know, wherever I am."

"You'll come running," Ian finished. He smiled at the angel. "Merry Christmas, Mike."

"Merry Christmas to you, too," Mike said.

Rosie turned to Mary. "I do think it's odd that Ian talks to himself that way," she whispered. "Do you think the smoke effected his brain somehow?"

In spite of herself, Mary laughed, and she shook her head. "No, I think he's fine," she said. "He's just speaking with Mike."

"Oh, that's right," Rosie said. "You know, it would be much easier to remember that he's in the room if he would just show himself." She paused for a moment. "Or perhaps he could wear a ribbon or a bell."

Ian glanced over at Mary and winked. "Aye," he agreed with Rosie. "Or, better yet, a tartan."

"I'm not wearing one of those Scottish skirts," Mike replied. Then he smiled at his friends. "I just don't have the legs for it."

Laughing, Ian walked over to Clarissa and squatted down next to her. "Merry Christmas, little darling," he said.

She threw her arms around his neck and hugged him. "Merry Christmas, Uncle Ian," she said. "I love you."

He smiled and kissed her cheek. "I love you, too," he said.

"When are you coming back?" she asked.

"Well, for sure I'll come when Mikey's born," he said. "And that's not too far away, is it?"

"Just three weeks away," Clarissa said. "And then I get to be a sister."

"That's amazing," he said. "I'll be back in three weeks then."

Clarissa peeked over her shoulder at her mom, then smiled at Ian. "Unless he's late," she said with a grin.

"Clarissa," Mary said with mock sternness. "I thought we discussed that we would never mention that option in this house."

Clarissa smiled widely. "Oh, I forgot," she teased.

"Good thing Santa is already on his way," Mary teased back. "Or you, young lady, would have a couple of coal lumps in your stocking."

Ian gave her one more quick hug and then stood, gathering his suitcase and coat. Mary walked him to the door. "I have the next shift," she said. "So, perhaps I'll see you again tonight."

"If not," he replied, "take care of yourself and Mikey." Then he lowered his voice and leaned in next to her. "And never, ever tell Bradley about what happened between you and Tony."

She nodded. "I agree," she said. "He'd probably take my Louisville Slugger away from me."

Ian studied her for a long moment. "At the very least," he said. He leaned forward and placed another kiss on her cheek. "Be well."

"You too," she replied. "And try to be happy."

Chapter Sixty-six

Mary walked down the deserted hospital hallway, the slap of her boots echoing against the tiled floor. There were signs of the holidays in the lobby and on office doors, but there was generally little joy in a hospital on Christmas Eve.

She reached the elevator bank and automatically pressed the button for the fourth floor. She had been up to Stanley's room so many times in the past few days that she could probably find her way in her sleep.

When the door closed, she leaned against the back wall. It had been an exhausting day, getting everything ready for their celebration tomorrow. She smiled fondly as she thought about Bradley struggling through the assembly instructions of Clarissa's Christmas gift. When she left, he was muttering some very unChristmas-like words. And, for some reason, he didn't seem to appreciate her reminder that Santa was listening.

Still chuckling when the door opened, her mood quickly shifted when she saw the look of the nurse on shift.

"Stanley?" she asked.

"He's had some respiratory issues tonight," she said. "His blood pressure has also been fluctuating, and his heart rate slowed."

"Should I get his wife?" Mary asked.

"I don't know," the nurse replied. "This could be his body giving up the fight, or it could be just a weird fluctuation. Why don't you go see him and then you can decide."

She hurried down the hall to his room. He was no longer in isolation, so they could actually sit next to his bed and talk to him. The door was slightly ajar, but the curtain had been drawn across it. She started to enter, then paused when she heard Ian's voice. He was softly singing to Stanley.

"And there's a hand, my trusty friend!

And give us a hand of yours!

And we'll take a deep draught of good-will

For long, long ago.

Should auld acquaintance be forgot,

And never brought to mind?

Should auld acquaintance be forgot,

And auld lang syne."

She quietly entered the room to find Ian crying softly at Stanley's bedside. He looked up when she came towards him. "He's naught but an old, grumpy coot," he whispered. "But he's the closest I've had to a da in a long time."

She pulled up a chair next to him and nodded. "I know," she said, placing his hand over hers. "Do you think we need to call Rosie?"

He took a deep breath, wiped his tears with his sleeve and nodded sadly. "Aye, I wouldna have her miss the last moments with him," he said. He stood up and nodded. "I'll make the call. You take some time with him."

She moved into the chair closest to Stanley and took his bandaged hand in hers. "Stanley," she whispered. "You can't give up. You have to fight. We need you here." Her voice cracked, and tears began to flow. "I need you here. You have to teach Mikey how to fish. You have to tell Clarissa about the old days. You have to be part of our family."

She laid her head down on the blanket and cried softly. "You can't die, Stanley," she wept softly. "Please God, don't let him die."

And then she smelled it again. Fresh pine and vanilla. She immediately sat up and saw that on the other side of Stanley's bed stood the Spirit of Christmas.

"It's midnight, Mary, on Christmas Eve," he said. "A time of miracles."

He looked down at Stanley and smiled kindly. "Even though he was a grumbler, he's always been on my good list," he said.

"You really have a list?" Mary whispered.

He laughed softly. "No, my dear, I don't," he replied. "But I do get to sometimes grant wishes. What would you like for Christmas, my dear?"

"Can you?" she stammered, afraid to hope. "Please. Save Stanley."

He smiled at her, and Mary felt his goodness fill her heart. "Blessed Christmas," he said, then he paused, put his hand in his pocket and placed something on the corner of the bed. "Oh, by the way, this is for Bradley."

When he lifted his hand, she saw a duplicate of the antique Christmas ornament that had been destroyed. She looked up to thank him but he was already gone.

Then Mary felt pressure on her hand and, in disbelief, looked up to see Stanley looking at her. He reached up, pulled the oxygen mask away from his face and grumbled, "How come I'm hooked up to all these dang-blasted contraptions?" he asked, his voice weak.

"Well, you've been a little sick," she said, beaming with joy.

"Humph," he replied. "I ain't been sick a day in my life. Must have been a misdiagnosis."

She bent over and kissed his forehead. "You're right," she said, wiping her tears away. "Must have been."

Ian entered the room and froze, staring at Stanley. "Well, look who finally decided to wake up," he said, his voice filled with emotion. "Stanley, I'm so happy to see those beady eyes of yours that I could kiss you on the mouth."

"Well, if that ain't the most disgusting thing I ever heard, I don't know what is," Stanley grumbled.

Ian laughed joyously. "Come to think of it," he said, "you're absolutely right."

Stanley sighed. "What's it take to get a meal around here?" he asked. "I feel like the front of my stomach and the back of my stomach are side by side."

"I'll call a nurse," Mary said. "And we'll get you some food." She stood and started toward the door. Then she stopped and turned. "By the way, Merry Christmas, Stanley."

Stanley's eyes widened. "It's Christmas? Already?" he asked. "Well, goldurn it. I haven't gone shopping yet."

"I think Rosie will forgive you this time," Ian said. "Besides, you'll be able to shop the sales now."

Chapter Sixty-seven

Ian put his bag down in his bedroom and walked over to the window to watch the snow drift down on the city of Chicago.

"A Christmas miracle," he said softly, his heart still full. "A perfect night for it."

He chuckled softly as he realized he was scanning the skies for a glimpse of Santa Claus and his sleigh. Then he recalled his conversation with Mary in the hallway outside of Stanley's room just before Ian had left.

"Santa Claus?" Ian repeated incredulously.

"Well, the Spirit of Christmas," Mary corrected. "But, I suppose, yes."

"So it was him all along? The second shadow, the scent of pine and vanilla?" he asked.

"I think Bradley's was gingerbread," Mary added. "Smells that remind us of Christmas."

He thought about it for a long moment. "Well, it makes sense if you consider that Tony murdered his family during his season," Ian said slowly. "Almost on his watch."

Mary nodded. "Okay, I can see that," she replied. "But tonight...with Stanley."

Ian smiled down at her. "Oh, well, that's easy," he said tenderly. "Mary O'Reilly Alden deserved a very special Christmas gift. You've done an amazing job this year. Perhaps Stanley was your Christmas bonus."

She grinned up at him. "I'll take it," she said. Then she sighed. "And how about you? What do you need for your Christmas gift?"

Ian stepped away from the window, Mary's question still echoing in his mind. What did he need for his Christmas gift?

He thought about the look on Rosie's face when she came into the hospital room to see her beloved husband awake and alert. Was that enough? Or the look on Stanley's face when Clarissa hugged him and told him she'd missed him? Or Bradley's unashamed tears when he hugged his old friend?

Weren't all of those enough of a Christmas miracle for him?

He heard a soft thud and turned back to his bed. Somehow the hand mirror Adeline had given to him had slipped out of the pocket and landed on the bed. He looked slowly around the room. He was too experienced to believe that was just an accident. But, he couldn't sense anything in the room.

Shaking his head, he walked over and picked up the mirror. He felt an immediate tingle of energy shoot up his arm, and he nearly dropped it. But he held on to it and studied it carefully. It was well-crafted, with woodland scenes interspersed with characters from the fae. It was ancient, and the mirror itself was slightly speckled with age.

"What am I afraid of?" he muttered. "I'm a scientist, after all. Shouldn't I put legend to the test?"

The silver was glowing in the darkness. Ian turned so he sheltered it from any ambient light from the window, but the glow remained.

"Magic mirror," he scoffed lightly and was about to put it down.

But he couldn't. He couldn't dismiss it that lightly.

"I'm afraid to have hope," he finally admitted softly. "I want to believe so badly."

He looked into the depths of the old mirror and softly said, "*Credendo vides.*"

His own reflection wavered before him and then suddenly, light was streaming from the inside of the mirror into his bedroom, like it was a window rather than a mirror. He gazed into the glass, awestruck by the beauty of the scene before him. Never had he seen such verdant greenery or vibrant blue skies. Never had he heard such beautiful bird songs. Even the wind in the trees seemed to carry its own melody.

Then he saw her, and his heart froze. She was wandering underneath a large tree, the dappled sun shining in her red hair as she moved between branches towards a path. She stopped at the path and studied it for a moment. Then he heard her cry, "Ian, please find me. I'm waiting for you."

The mirror darkened, and the window was closed. Ian brought the mirror to his chest and closed his eyes. "I'll find you, darling," he whispered. "I promise I'll find you."

The End

(To learn more about the story of Ian and Gillian, read the Order of Brigid's Cross, Book Two, available in autumn of 2017.)

About the author: Terri Reid lives near Freeport, the home of the Mary O'Reilly Mystery Series, and loves a good ghost story. An independent author, Reid uploaded her first book "Loose Ends – A Mary O'Reilly Paranormal Mystery" in August 2010. By the end of 2013, "Loose Ends" had sold over 200,000 copies. She has sixteen other books in the Mary O'Reilly Series, the first books in the following series - "The Blackwood Files," "The Order of Brigid's Cross," and "The Legend of the Horsemen." She also has a stand-alone romance, "Bearly in Love." Reid has enjoyed Top Rated and Hot New Release status in the Women Sleuths and Paranormal Romance category through Amazon US. Her books have been translated into Spanish, Portuguese and German and are also now also available in print and audio versions. Reid has been quoted in several books about the self-publishing industry including "Let's Get Digital" by David Gaughran and "Interviews with Indie Authors: Top Tips from Successful Self-Published Authors" by Claire and Tim Ridgway. She was also honored to have some of her works included in A. J. Abbiati's book "The NORTAV Method for Writers – The Secrets to Constructing Prose Like the Pros."

She loves hearing from her readers at author@terrireid.com

Other Books by Terri Reid:

Mary O'Reilly Paranormal Mystery Series:

Mary O'Reilly Short Stories

The Order of Brigid's Cross (Sean's Story)

The Wild Hunt (Book 1)

The Blackwood Files (Art's Story)

File One: Family Secrets

File Two: Private Wars

PRCD Case Files: The Ghosts Of New Orleans -A Paranormal Research and Containment Division Case File

Eochaidh: Legend of the Horseman (Book One)

Sweet Romances

Bearly in Love

Sneakers – A Swift Romance

24072759R00175

Printed in Great Britain
by Amazon